Nigel Williar[illegible] educated at H[illegible] College, Oxford. His first novel, *My Life Closed Twice*, was published in 1977 and was joint winner of the Somerset Maugham Award. A second novel, *Jack Be Nimble*, appeared in 1980. A short play, *Double Talk*, was seen at the Square One Theatre, London, in 1976, and a television play, *Talkin' Blues*, on BBC-2 in 1977. For his first full-length stage play, *Class Enemy* (Royal Court Theatre, London, 1978), he was jointly named the year's most promising playwright. *Class Enemy* continues to be performed internationally, with great success. His next three stage plays were all seen in London during 1980: *Trial Run* (Young Vic); *Line 'Em* (National Theatre); *Sugar and Spice* (Royal Court). A television play, *Babylove*, was transmitted by the BBC in 1981, and a further stage play, *W.C.P.C.*, was first presented at the Half Moon Theatre, London, in 1982. In 1983 his third novel was published, *Johnny Jarvis*, drawn from his own television series. *Charlie* was first screened on ITV in March and April 1984.

Nigel Williams is married with three children and lives in London.

by the same author

FICTION
My Life Closed Twice
Jack Be Nimble
Johnny Jarvis

PLAYS
Class Enemy
Sugar and Space & Trial Run
Line 'Em
W.C.P.C.

NIGEL WILLIAMS

Charlie

METHUEN · LONDON

First published in Great Britain in 1984
as a Methuen Paperback original
by Methuen London Ltd,
11 New Fetter Lane, London EC4P 4EE

ISBN 0 413 55570 4

Printed in Great Britain
by Cox & Wyman Ltd, Reading

This publication is based on
the four-part television serial Charlie
produced by Central Productions
for Central Independent Television plc.

PART ONE

When I reached the fourth floor landing, I thought I heard a scream. I stopped and listened for a while. There was no other noise in the whole block apart from the wind on the bleak stone stairs, but, from the other end of the corridor that led away from the stairs, I heard footsteps. They were going the other way from me. The footsteps were what made me stay where I was. They went a few yards, then stopped, then started again. For some reason, the slow, deliberate noise they made frightened me. When I think about what happened afterwards – which I do quite a lot – the whole history seems contained in the insistent, cautious, echoing tread, half heard on a cold November night in a tower block on an estate in South London.

I pushed back the double doors that separated the landing from the corridor. All I saw was, thirty yards away from me, the one neon strip-light left on this floor. Before it and beyond it everything was in shadow, but it was easy to see that, shaded or lit, this corridor, like the one above it and below it, like the one I'd just left, like the whole estate, had the grim anonymity of a prison landing. A prison made all the more frightening by the fact that the inmates seemed to have access to Pentels, spray paints, knives, pencils, all sort of instruments with which to blazon their messages of despair and defiance.

The other side of the neon light, someone had left a door open and light was spilling out from it on to the steel grey floor and walls, curiously warm in that cold place. Something – probably the immediate memory of those footsteps, made me move on down towards it, hearing my own metallic tread, as fitful and circumspect as those I had heard earlier. Each yellow door, closed against the night, confirmed the anonymity and loneliness of the building. There were no sounds of singing, arguing, crying, no trace of human life at all coming from any one of the flats . . . 39 . . . 40 . . . 41 . . . . But gradually, as I grew closer, I heard the sound of an American voice. It was talking about the number of dead, and behind it I heard the whirr of helicopter wings. Someone had left the television on inside the flat with the open door. They had left it on very, very loud.

As soon as I got inside I realised the man was talking about Vietnam, and for a moment had one of those odd, displaced jolts, suffered from the brief illusion of travel through time and space that our world is always granting us. Then I realised I had been listening to one of those retrospectives. The hall of the flat seemed at first glance unremarkable. There was a table with some magazines on it, some official-looking wallpaper, and a battered chair against one wall. It looked more like an office than a private house. What drew me on, and regulated my tread to that same, wary rhythm in which it had begun, was the voice on the television: ' . . . sustaining an unacceptable level of casualties on the ground . . . civilian deaths due to air strike . . . at this time impossible to say or predict what eventually . . . ' I went on towards the cream door and pushed it open, as fearfully as a child alone in a house at night.

I saw him straight away. He was lying in the centre of the carpet, around him the wreckage of a table, papers, glasses, a broken bottle, a smear of magazines. From his head, in a long, sickle shaped curve was a giant, red stain. The blood was on his face too, on his shirtfront, and on his hands that clawed the carpet as if it had been the face of his assailant. But it was far too late for any of that. Whoever had done him had done a very good job indeed.

When I went over to him I assumed he was dead. I put

my face down to his and it was only then I saw that his lips were moving. They were silently opening and closing as if in prayer. I put my hand on his shoulder and leaned into his face. It wasn't a prepossessing face. Even in agony or death, this face had an angry, awkward expression, narrow eyes, lips as thin as a pencil mark, and –

He was trying to say something. I leaned even closer. Then, like the rustle of a distant train on the steel rails of a station, I heard his voice, coming from a long way away, the voice of a dying man, the sort of voice that does not quite belong to its owner. I listened hard. Sometimes I thought he was saying: 'name . . . name . . . ', and then: 'numb . . . numb . . . numb . . . '. Then I arranged the shapes of his voice into two words, until those two words were the only thing to match the ceaseless, soft chatter of the thin lips. 'Knew him . . . knew him . . . *knew* him . . . . '

The last two words were articulated with a sudden force and clearness that, at first, I mistook for signs of life. Then as the man stiffened and fell back I saw that only one thing had produced this brief animation. What had driven him to the point of clarity – or what looked like clarity – was nothing more than hatred. Looking at his eyes, narrowing down like a television screen last thing at night, I was reminded of another dying man, years ago, when I was in the Army. Some stupid drunk had knocked him off his motor bike near our barracks, and I was the first one to him. Over and over again, all he said, before he died, was 'the bastard . . . the bastard . . . '.

I was thinking about that man when Stanley Peace went limp in my arms, stopped trying to speak and coughed, a long, ghastly cough. Stanley Peace was the third person I had seen die – if you count my father – and, unlike my father, he died in my arms. Nice for him.

I let the body down on to the carpet and went for the phone. The police, as usual, did not seem to be answering

999 calls. Maybe they were all at a lacrosse match. Eventually a more than usually stupid desk sergeant picked up the line and I began the difficult task of explaining to him, in words of one and two syllables that I had found a dead man on the Wearing Estate. I was half-way through this task, when, immediately below me, I saw the address book. I don't know what made me pick it up. Idle curiosity. I saw on the inside cover that the book belonged to someone called Stan Peace, but that was not what made me shut the book, drop the phone and run for the corridor. What I'd seen was my own name on the first page. You see I had never seen this man before in my life. And he'd even spelt my name right: Charlie, with an 'ie'.

It was when I was out in the corridor that I heard the footsteps again. But this time it was a brief flurry, a clatter, then a panicked scramble for the landing at the other end of the corridor. I lowered my head and ran for the far doors. When I burst through them into the freezing night I saw nothing apart from the lights of the estate, piled stories high about the arterial road. There was a stone staircase at the other end of this open landing, but that, too, was deserted. Whoever was out there was in a lot better condition than me. Far away, down on the estate road I saw the lights of a car, reverse out, turn, and burn their way back towards the main drag. I opened the address book once again. There it was –

CHARLIE ALEXANDER – 777–987

Then, from the direction taken by the leaving car I saw the blue light of the police van. I lit a cigarette and, slowly, descended the open staircase towards the empty wastes that lie between the giant buildings in that part of the city.

Now I come to think of it, it was probably the Venables business that had brought me to the Wearing estate that night. Venables was a creature who had worked his way into my list of clients by actually managing to see my ad in the *Wandsworth News*. I had a special fondness for him because he had managed to find that advert in among the used cars and almost-new kitchen units that surrounded it. I think Venables was almost the only example I can call to mind of business created by what I described to Susan as my 'sales drive'.

'Are you a Private Eye?' he said to me on our first meeting.

I jumped slightly at this description. It sounded impossibly glamorous.

'Sort of . . . ,' I said guardedly.

'I expect you have to keep it quiet,' said Venables, sagely.

Actually I am a journalist. Or was. I'm nothing really. I am a thirty-eight year old mess. But if it makes you feel better to describe me as a Private Eye, feel free to do so.

Venables, like a lot of the people who rang Information Services, apart from the ones who wanted translations done from the Swedish, or blocked drains cleared, wanted me to find his ex-wife. I don't think I ever found her.

For some reason I didn't look at the address book that night. I went back to the flat and locked it in a drawer. Just the thought of my name in the dead man's book, sleeping there, like some whispered opinion by a close friend who has become an enemy, made me nervous. I sat at the window, smoked, and read my farewell letter from Susan. It was, you had to admit, a good letter. It was a little too influenced by Scott Fitzgerald, but it had a nice easy ring to it. The subordinate clauses were all in the right place, and, in the last paragraph, there was even a joke, which I thought was a nice touch. Charlie is a jokey bloke you see. Wry, laconic, you know the sort of thing. What made it especially hurtful was that the joke was one of mine. Susan had a way of appropriating my mannerisms and turns of speech, as if such things were not, and never could be, individual.

' . . . What Saul can give me now is something I suppose I never thought I would have, something, as an adolescent, all those years ago, I suppose I was chasing . . . . '

Perhaps she was going to make a collected edition of her brush-off letters and have it published by Virago to enormous public acclaim. I folded the letter very neatly and put it in the drawer next to the address book. Then I went to bed. My last thought before I fell asleep was a familiar one. What is it (apart from the obvious) that Saul *can* give her? If it had been a wrestler, or a trombonist or a parachutist I think I could have understood it. But an estate agent. An *estate agent*.

'Darling,' said Maggie the next morning, 'is it Cock? Is that all it is? Because if it's just Cock, she'll be back. I've had it when it's just Cock, and it's *no good*.'

Maggie is my neighbour. We're on good terms. She describes herself as a literary agent, but, as far as I can see has no clients.

'It's because he's tender,' I said, 'and gentle and understanding. He understands how she feels and she understands how he feels.'

'It is just Cock,' said Maggie.

She was wearing a kind of purple kimono, with what looked like a pair of Hush Puppies. I decided to tell her about the address book.

'What do you *do* exactly Charlie?' she said, when I'd finished.

I curled my lip slightly and said, 'I'm a Private Eye.'

She found this extremely funny for some reason. We finished our coffee, and she departed for what she described as a 'meeting', or, as we say, a bottle of sherry.

When she'd gone I walked around the room a few times and phoned a man who had asked me to prepare a 'consultative document' on the Arms Race. It turned out he'd asked someone else to prepare a consultative document as well, and this guy, unlike me, had actually managed to produce one. Not only that – it sounded, from my man's description – to be a first-class example of the genre.

'Why,' I said to him, 'did you ask for two consultative documents? Was it a race?'

He hung up.

My eyes kept coming back to the drawer. In the end I got out the book.

Stanley Peace had known a lot of people. There were nearly a hundred pages in the volume and each page was packed with names, numbers and addresses, all transcribed in the same remorselessly neat writing. I didn't really look at any of them. I kept coming back to my name, on the first page of the book. It was that, I think, that made me decide to phone the name at the head of the page. The entry read simply,

AINSWORTH, HARRY.D.W.U. NUMBER – 097–6321.

I think what made me call that name was that, although, otherwise, the pages seemed arranged in alphabetical order, this name had been chosen to lead. Perhaps the otherwise systematic Mr. Peace had thought this person more than usually important. After three rings a voice said, 'Distributive Workers' Union!'

The voice said this in a pleased way, as if talking to very young children.

I said, in my relaxed 'journalist' voice, 'Harry Ainsworth please.'

'Who is that calling him?'

'Alexander,' I said, 'Charlie Alexander.'

There was a click, and, alarmingly close, a Northern voice, said, 'Ainsworth.'

I started my spiel about Information Services. I was a freelance organisation providing information on a freelance basis, working not only to newspapers or television companies but to any individual or organisation that needed factual background on a complex issue of the moment, political, artistic or technical, tailored to their immediate 'communication needs'. I was particularly proud of the last phrase, combining as it did, euphony with lack of meaning in a uniquely astringent way. I ended with my joke.

'If you want facts try a computer. But I come *with* a computer.'

I always did intend buying a computer actually. But I've never got round to understanding how they work.

Mr. Ainsworth did not evince any of the more typical responses to the Information Services spiel – laughter, incomprehension or direct rudeness. He waited until I had ground to a halt and said,

'Come to my office. 3.30. Carshalt Road. District Office. I expect Stan told you where to find it.'

I gulped.

'Right,' I said, 'it's –.'

'By Campbell Grove. Clapham.'

I groped for the A–Z as he rang off, wondering why, all of a sudden, Charles Alexander was becoming popular.

I had no trouble in finding the place. Carshalt Road was only a hundred yards long. At the far end of it was a small, brick building, that looked like a cross between an air-raid shelter and a urinal. Above the front door was a sign that read DISTRIBUTIVE WORKERS' UNION, and underneath that, in quotation marks, 'IN UNION IS STRENGTH'. Without quite knowing how I was going to introduce myself I marched up to the entrance and grasped the handle of the door firmly. As I did so, a small, ferret-like woman appeared, framed in the glass panel in front of me. She tugged the door back violently and grinned.

'Coom in, Mr. Alexander.'

Why, I wondered, did all the members of the Distributive Workers' Union (whatever that might be) have Northern accents?

The woman showed me in to an office-cum-reception area that reminded me of a station waiting room. She looked like secretaries used to look. She even had a pair of glasses shaped like truncated hearts. They gave her a Gothic look belied by her open face and even more open accent.

'He'll not be long,' she said. 'It's Mr. Alexander isn't it?'

She grinned at me in a conspiratorial tone as she said this. She seemed to know more about me than I did. I tried to remember some key facts about the Trade Union Movement.

'Is Mr. Ainsworth a Convenor?' I said, eventually.

The woman looked shocked.

'Mr. Ainsworth', she said, in a somewhat aggrieved voice, 'is District Organiser.'

I nodded wisely. There were a lot of posters on the wall telling me about rights I never knew I had. Eventually the phone on the secretary's desk buzzed and she received what sounded like instructions to show me upstairs.

As we climbed the stairs, that led up to a small landing, off which were two heavy doors, on one of which was written MR H. AINSWORTH, I wondered, out loud, where the other members of the D.W.U. might be.

'This is only the District Office,' said the woman, 'on Fridays it's packed.'

'They have music then, do they?'

She decided not to answer this, but showed me in to a large, pleasant room, at the end of which was a desk. Behind the desk was a man who gave the impression of attempting, without much success, to be as large and pleasant as the room. He was of medium build, with a brick red face and a handshake of such effusive normality that I was at once suspicious of him.

'Two coffees, Laura love,' he said.

The woman ducked and left. As I went to sit down I got a closer look at Mr. Ainsworth.

The most notable thing about him was his suit. It looked as if it had come from a Jugoslav version of Burton's. It was only outdone by his shoes, which were like *objets trouvés* from the same shop. The other notable thing was his hair. He had brushed what was left of it up into two tufts, either side of his ears, which gave him the appearance of a pantomime devil. It was the hair, more than anything, that made me suspect the sprightly, down-to-earth manner, so that, after a few minutes, I found myself wondering whether the accent might not be assumed, whether the man was not acting the part of a hopelessly antiquated trades unionist for some devious reasons of his own.

'Any friend of Stan's', Ainsworth was saying, 'is a friend of mine. How are things out at Fairlie's?'

'Oh,' I said, hoping I looked more informed than I felt, 'they're . . . . '

'They're disastrous aren't they?' he went on. 'Nice little engineering firm, nice little airfield there, just off the South Circular, whip down the A22 ten minutes you're in Bewick you're there. It *must* be bloody viable don't you think?'

I nodded keenly, hoping the conversation would proceed along these lines for the foreseeable future. Perhaps he would start handing out maps.

'Stan's done bloody wonders out there,' he said, 'bloody best steward we ever bloody had out there I bloody tell you.'

'Bloody right,' I said.

He looked up at me sharply.

'What was it you wanted to see me about,' he said.

I reflected that, in effect, it was he who had wanted to see me, but did not say so.

'Stan Peace,' I said, letting my fingers tighten round the address book.

'Aye,' he said, 'I thought it might be.'

I looked at the wall behind him. There was a poster on which was a picture of a girl in a white dress. Above her were written the words COME TO BULGARIA. I decided to give Mr. Ainsworth a surprise.

'He's dead,' I said.

I thought he was going to cry. He hunched up inside his suit, like a little old man. I felt sorry for him. Not that what I said next was calculated to make him feel any better. I told him about the estate and the flat and how I had found my name in the address book. Mr. Ainsworth did not appear to listen to any of this. He sat staring at me, like a man who has been sentenced to death. When I had finished he said, in a flat voice,

'Who put Stan on to you?'

'I rather intended to ask you that question,' I said.

'Somebody gave your name to Stan Peace,' said Ainsworth slowly. 'Stan told me about it. All about it. Is that what you spend your life doing? Hanging around embassies waiting for a few crumbs of – '

'What are you talking about?' I said, 'who is this person who gave my name to – '

Ainsworth got to his feet.

'GO DOWN TO BLOODY FAIRLIE'S AND TELL HIM I HAVEN'T GOT ANYTHING FOR HIM YOU HEAR?' he screamed. 'TELL HIM I'M BLOODY THROUGH WITH IT, O.K?'

At this moment the secretary appeared at the door. She carried a rather homey looking tray on which were a jug, some biscuits and two cups and saucers. Ainsworth turned to her.

'This young man,' he said, 'is called Alexander. On no

account are you to either take his calls or allow him anywhere near the inside of this building.'

I rose, as gracefully as is possible when people have been shouting at you. He still hadn't finished though.

'If it wasn't that bastard at Fairlie's it must have been a friend of his,' he said, 'I want to know who – '

He was still asking questions as I walked out onto the landing. I didn't see why I should stay in the room, when there were plenty of questions of my own that needed asking. I didn't think I'd get any sense out of him anyway. He looked like a man in the middle of a nervous breakdown. Maybe the suit was getting him down.

I think I would have left the whole thing there, if it hadn't been for the car that followed me as I pulled away from Carshalt Road. Whoever was inside the vehicle had clearly learned their techniques of surveillance from old Hollywood films. He was following the two basic rules – Stay Three Cars Behind and Look Sinister. He did look quite ridiculously sinister. At least in the driving mirror he did. It was that that decided me to head for the South Circular. After all, it was only since I'd found this damned address book that people had started shouting inexplicable things at me. Maybe it was responsible for my being followed as well.

What puzzled me was why Mr. Ainsworth should have wanted to see me at all, and why his attitude to me had depreciated so rapidly on his being informed that Stanley Peace had had his head bashed in. Did he think I'd done it? As I pushed the Cortina into third gear, and turned into Balham High Street I went over what he had said again. He appeared to want to know who had given my name to Peace, which implied the thing was as much of a mystery to him as it was to me, but he seemed to be saying that he had a very good idea of *why* my name had ended up in that address book.

'Who,' I said to the dashboard, 'is the Bastard at Fairlie's? Is he like the Hunchback of Notre Dame? And why is somebody following me?'

As if in response I saw the sinister man, religiously keeping three cars behind, grimace in a sinister fashion. Maybe he had been sent to frighten me by the Inland Revenue.

By the time I got on to the A22, the man behind me had given up. Or, I thought idly, got better at following people without being seen. Bewick turned out to be one of those non-places common on the roads out of London to the South, and, as I drove past the sign that told me I was in it, I saw another off to the right telling me it was three miles to Fairlie's Aerodrome and Industrial Park.

It was raining as I turned off the main road and drove up past a park, a church and a school, all of which had a vaguely under-used air. At the brow of the hill the landscape suddenly changed from toytown-suburban and had a go at rurality, without conspicuous success. I passed a field of cabbages, a group of rather dingy looking meadows, and then, at the edge of the limited horizon, I saw the dull green spaces of an airfield.

Mr. Ainsworth, I felt, had been a touch complimentary in his description of the place. There was nothing nice about the barbed wire fence, the broken boards or the gaunt buildings heaped together at the end of one runway. The rain added to the gloom, sweeping in from the fields beyond, spattering against the sign that swung above me as I drove past the huge, metal gates that opened off the road. FOR SALE: VACANT OFFICE SPACE 7000 SQUARE METRES. Another place closing.

The buildings, when you were close to them, were really two huge sheds, separated by a hundred yards, around which clustered a collection of makeshift buildings that reminded me of some South American shanty town. Both looked utterly deserted. I parked the car as close as I could, and, pulling my jacket round me, ran towards the nearest of the two buildings.

There were no doors. Or, if there had been doors they had been removed, along with the furniture, the floor and what equipment the place had once contained. I found I was gazing into what looked like a roofed in parade ground. In the centre, seated round an upturned packing case were a group of men in blue overalls, playing cards. All of them, I decided, as I approached, qualified for the title 'The Bastard of Fairlie's'. They were, to a man, squat, furtive and unprepossessing. Maybe they didn't like being up for sale.

I'm a big bloke, about six four, and some people have found me, to my surprise, a touch menacing, but I tried to keep my voice sweet and light, as I said,

'I want to talk to someone about Stan Peace.'

'You the Law?'

'No.'

'Insurance?'

'No.'

'Don't have to talk to you then do we?'

Well someone had told *them* anyway. Looking at the four of them I decided they were all quite definitely suspects. I went closer to the makeshift table.

'I should raise him four and see him,' I said to the one nearest to me.

'Fuck off,' he said.

The one opposite him, a fattish man of about forty, looked up from his hand, cautiously.

'You from the Union?' he said.

'That's it.'

'Well you want Dave don't you then,' he said.

The others seemed to find this uproariously funny.

'Dave who?'

'Dave Abbott. Only he's off at a bloody conference isn't he? All they ever do is to go conferences. That's why this is up for the knackers.'

'So Dave was a friend of Stan's then . . . ,' I said.

'Of course he bloody was,' said the fattish man. 'I thought you said you were – '

'I am,' I said. 'I am.'

This was not going to get me very far, and, with the sort of cheery wave I hoped was typical of officials of the Distributive Workers' Union, I headed back towards the grey afternoon. What was I doing in this godforsaken place? Maybe Stan Peace had seen my ad in the *Wandsworth News*. Maybe he too had lost his wife. I was on the point of resolving to ignore the presence of my name in the book and the curious behaviour of Mr. Ainsworth, when I reached the mouth of the building and looked across at my car.

I knew at once what he was looking for. I cursed myself for being such a fool as to leave the thing in the car. But before I was half-way there, the man who had been following me earlier was legging it across the aerodrome and, even from this distance I could see that in his right hand was the small red notebook. He didn't look quite as sinister as he had done earlier, but as I pounded after him, he revealed an unsuspected talent for running. His car was parked round the side of the second building, and I caught him just as he reached it. I pulled his left arm and swung him against the windscreen as hard as I could. This did not seem to have much effect on him. He bounced back at me, grunting something, and butted me in the chest. Winded, I groped for his right hand, which still held the address book, and for a moment thought I had it. Then he tore away from me and was fumbling with his keys in the front seat of his car. I got up and reached inside, just as he started the engine. My hand was on his face, clawing and squeezing, as he accelerated away across the damp, uneven grass.

I was all right until he reached the runway. Then he put the thing into second gear and was up to twenty miles an hour before I had the chance to put the Charlie Alexander Home Commando Defeat Your Enemy With The First Three Fingers Of The Right Hand Technique into operation. He yanked the wheel round to the right and I was thrown clear as he roared off towards those huge, metal gates. I looked down at my right hand. It was bleeding. In it was a scrap of paper. When I looked at it closely I saw it was the first half of the first page of the late Mr. Stanley Peace's address book.

'Nobody messes around with Charlie Alexander,' I said, in an American accent. I said it again later, in the car. It made me feel a little more like a private detective. If things went on like this, I decided, I would hire one to protect *me* – a lean, tough, fearless, cigarette-smoking private dick. As things stood, I wasn't entirely sure that I was going to be quite enough.

I saw Susan in the supermarket in Barnes High Street the next day, and I asked her whether I knew anyone called Stan Peace.

'Don't ask me,' she said. 'I don't work for the company any more.'

I am a limited company. That dates from the days when I earned quite a lot of money as a freelance journalist. Susan couldn't understand why I gave all that up.

'You were independent weren't you?' she used to say.

'Sure,' I said, 'I was free to do what I was told.'

She would snort at that remark and say something about my being quixotic. I took that as a compliment. But Susan and I, for the moment anyway, were behaving with the circumspect politeness of people at the funeral of a distant acquaintance.

'What are you up to?' she said.

'Investigating a murder,' I said, with quiet pride.

She choked back her obvious disbelief and tried to look as if I'd made some more normal comment. Then our act fell apart rather, as Ben and Toby wandered up, both heavily armed with plastic weapons. It is when I see them that I start to hate her again. I can't explain that. Perhaps I don't like the awful way my children lay me open. I can't, though I have tried, hold back the embarrassing public nature of my love for them. I bent down and kissed Ben. He didn't seem to object, but I noticed Susan doing practical things with her shoulders. She gestured towards a small fat child seated next to the counter. I would have put its age at about eighteen months, but its huge jowls and bleary, downcast air gave it the look of someone immensely older and sadder and wiser.

'If you want to have something to do with your children,' she said tightly, 'you could hold Rupert for me.'

Rupert, I thought. My God, we called him Rupert. Why did we do that?

I picked him up anway as she shovelled avocados and baby cream and chicken pieces into her bag. I took him over to the plate glass window of the supermarket, and held him up so as he could see the bright winter morning. He started to struggle, feebly, like a fish on its last gasp, and one fat hand began to gesture to the street. I followed the line of it and saw Saul, climbing out of his BMW. Saul looks like one of those TV heroes in a West Coast detective series. He got out of the car now and scanned the street keenly, then he swayed hippily towards the shop. He's trying, I thought, *not to look like an estate agent*. I glanced back at Susan, who was still packing things into her bag.

'You knew some very left-wing people at Oxford,' she said.

Methodical girl Susan. Great loss to the company.

'But in a trades *union* . . . . '

Then Saul came in. His eyes went straight to Ben, and he opened his arms to my son in a Jewish-Italian gesture.

'Benny . . . ' he said.

Ben seemed to think this was fine. Grinning he ran to Saul and allowed himself to be picked up and swirled round. Saul fancies himself with children.

'He's just a great big kid himself really isn't he?' I said to Susan.

She came over to me and took Rupert out of my arms.

'Don't be stupid Charlie.'

They had started out of the shop. It was funny. When Susan and I were together any journey involving the children, even one of two or three yards, was always accompanied by screams, yells, detours and hysteria. Saul shepherded the four of them towards the car like a courier, long used to such manoeuvres.

'I don't get it,' I said. 'He's incredibly good looking, he's wonderful with children, he's an estate agent. He's got a chest wig. Where do I come in?'

'You don't Charlie,' said Susan.

I watched the car as it roared off towards the river. The children didn't turn back to wave. I expect Saul was already telling them one of his marvellous, impromptu stories, or producing Star Wars men out of thin air, or –

God damn Saul. May he rot in hell.

I looked at myself in the window of the supermarket. I needed cheering up. I went into the Coach and Horses and had two pints of lager. When I came out I still looked as if I needed cheering up only now I had a red face as well. I went up to the library on Castelnau. I decided I needed to know more about the Distributive Workers' Union.

When I asked the woman on the desk if she had any books about trades unions, she gave me a narrow stare. I felt as if I had asked after works of child pornography.

'I'll see,' she said darkly.

They had four books about trades unions. None of them had been taken out. In fact, judging from the slips on the inside cover, none of them had *ever* been taken out. They had snappy titles like *The Theory and Practice of Trades Union Legislation in a Modern Society.* One of them was a history book. The last was called *The Horizon Guide to Modern British Trades Unions.* It appeared to be intended for schoolchildren. As it was the only one I could understand I took it over to a table by the window, watched closely by the woman on the desk. She clearly expected me to produce a whistle and start recruiting her to a Marxist-Leninist workers organisation at any moment.

At the back of the book was an index. It had two lines on the Distributive Workers' Union. The D.W.U. (as those in the know clearly liked to call it) had approx. 40,000 members, represented semi-skilled workers mainly in the engineering industry and had been formed in 1910 out of a coalition between the Amalgamated Society of Harbour and Dock Employees and the Engineering Employees' Federation. Its head offices were somewhere in Croydon and its Ann. Conf. was held in November in Eastbourne.

'All right Charles,' I said to myself, 'we'll go to the seaside.'

In Eastbourne in November the old people still come out to pace up and down the seafront. I suppose they suspect each day might be the last chance they get to look at the pier, the empty beach, and the sun, low and pale on the horizon. I felt quite at home there.

The Distributive Workers held their annual conference in something called the Empire Leisure Halls, a cavernous building that uniquely combines the atmosphere of a prison and a swimming bath. They had hung streamers and flags across it, and in the foyer were crowds of earnest young men selling newspapers with titles like *Strife* or *Pledge*, but it still looked like a cross between a swimming bath and a prison.

I told the woman on the desk I worked for the BBC. She seemed to like that. Telling people you work for the BBC is a bit like arriving on a bicycle. They feel sorry for you and anxious to help. They never seem to expect you to carry a Press card. I went through to the hall and slipped into a plastic chair behind a table marked Press. Nobody paid me any attention. A man up on the platform was talking about Rule 87a and asking whether it had been complied with in this case. I leaned over to the man immediately next to me. He had a thick handlebar moustache, and looked more like an RAF officer than a journalist.

'Have you seen Dave Abbott?' I said.

The man looked at me blankly.

'Who he?' he said.

'He steward at Fairlie's,' I said.

He pushed a small booklet at me. It was entitled LIST OF DELEGATES TO ANNUAL CONFERENCE EASTBOURNE NOVEMBER 1984. Dave Abbott's name was at the head of the list, with an indecipherable set of initials next to it. I showed it to the man with the moustache, who brightened immediately at the sight of the letters.

'I know him,' he said. 'Area 24. He's over there . . . .'

And he pointed towards the far side of the hall.

One of the things that had made me determined to travel as far as Eastbourne to meet Mr. Abbott was the fact that, although he had worked at the same place as Mr. Peace, had been a member of the same union even, he had not appeared, as far as I could tell, in the address book. Why was that? He ought to have been on the first page. I got up and wandered across the hall to where the man with the moustache had pointed. It was lucky, I reflected that members of the D.W.U. seemed to go around with large badges on their lapels telling you who they were. In fact, the whole affair reminded me of one of those American conventions rather than a dangerous left-wing conspiracy. Whatever the members were like, the delegates certainly looked more like middle-range executives of a large corporation than anything else.

I walked down the side of the hall, scanning the lapels to right and left of me. Then, just as I was getting uncomfortably close to the platform, a small bronzed man rose up in my path, on his way out of the place. I caught a glimpse of a regular profile, a neat blue shirt and then I saw DAVID ABBOTT. FAIRLIE'S S.C. Before he slipped past me, I grabbed him by the arm.

'Mr. Abbott,' I said, 'I need to talk to you about Stan Peace.'

He stopped.

'You are?'

I wondered which lie to tell him.

'I'm a private detective,' I said.

I didn't say this in an American accent. In fact, it didn't seem, as I said it, as much like a lie as, say, 'I'm a freelance journalist' or 'I'm an unemployed graduate'.

He seemed impressed by it. He didn't roll around the floor laughing, or ask me what precisely I detected, or, worst of all, ask for my licence (I suppose to be a proper private detective you do need a licence?). He stepped back slightly, and looked cautious. Well of course, if I *was* a private detective, he would need to look cautious wouldn't he?

'Come and get a coffee,' he said.

The man up on the platform had finished talking about Rule 87a and had gone on to the infinitely more riveting subject of Rule 23c. I looked back at him, a foursquare, red-faced man of about fifty.

'What's got into him?' I said.

'That's our general secretary,' said Abbott, 'Owen Harris. Left-winger.'

I tried to look interested. Abbott steered us both towards a large trestle table on which was a collection of battered urns. Behind the table was a woman in blue overalls, knitting with passionate concentration. Abbott passed me a coffee and looked up at the platform. He seemed to be enjoying the spectacle.

'They won't take this,' he said.

'Why not?'

'There's a nasty about Cruise tacked on to it. From Bristol. Very far to the right is Bristol.'

In front of Mr. Owen Harris, from the seats in the body of the hall, a tall, pinched-looking man was waving his arms and shouting. Abbott seemed to gain pleasure from this as well.

'There goes Prothero,' he said.

'Who's Prothero?'

'Prominent right-winger. Lost out on the last election. *Hates* Harris.'

It was all beginning to seem a bit like the Mafia. I watched as Prothero continued to wave his arms. He was talking about Rule 51d. There seemed to be a lot of rules in the Distributive Workers' Union. I sipped at my coffee and wondered why Mr. Abbott was being so accommodating. Then from over to the left of Mr. Prothero I saw my friend Mr. Ainsworth. He was in shirt sleeves, and he too was shouting. He seemed to have discovered a rule all of his own and he was very excited about it. So was the man on the platform. As if in answer to my unspoken thought of a moment earlier, Abbot said,

'I'd like to help you all I can. I take it you want to know who killed him.'

I was disconcerted by the directness of this response.

'You were a friend of his, Mr. Abbott?'

'A colleague.'

The man on the platform seemed to be in agreement with my mate Ainsworth. The man called Prothero was now shouting that he had been treated with contempt in this matter. Abbott watched all this with a sleepy grin.

'Stan would have loved all of this.'

'Yes?'

'Meat and drink to Stan this was.'

'Now tell me, Stan was left . . . or right?'

'Hard line Stalinist.'

'Ah.'

Mr. Ainsworth's rule, it had been decided, was the best of all possible rules. The people who were able to decide this, I noticed, were the people behind the table on the platform, and the man who knew, by some mystical process of intuition that this was what the people behind the table wanted, was the red-faced, foursquare Mr. Owen Harris. Somebody was suggesting that lunch be taken. The conference settle in to debate this urgent question with the keenness of men engaged in some mediaeval theological discussion. Abbott and I drifted out into the hall. He nodded to people as we passed in that same, easy, confident manner. I noticed he had protuberant blue eyes and a slightly alarming, contained energy about him, rather like a man whose thyroid is moving too fast. He looked, I decided, like a ladies' man.

'Stan', he went on, 'thought that Bulgaria was the only place.'

'Yes?'

'Look – are you working for Ella?'

'I'm sorry?'

'Did Stan's wife hire you?'

'I didn't know he had a wife.'

Then, because I had started being honest with him, I told him what had happened to me without too many alterations. He listened to the story of the address book and the incident at the airfield without interruption, then he said,

'I'll see you by the pier. Eleven tomorrow morning. I'd like to help you.'

As if I had been part of what was happening all around me and not some stranger, he dived off into the crowd to greet another fellow trades unionist, abandoning me to the flow of respectable looking men in suits, on their way out into the foyer of the place.

There wasn't much to do in Eastbourne except think. I thought about Mr. Abbott quite a lot. I thought about Ainsworth too. It seemed impossible to credit that they were members of the same organisation. I spent the evening in a pub reading literature filched from the conference, including a copy of a rulebook I'd found under the Press table. The one thing the rulebook didn't mention was what seemed – as far as I could see – to be the most important thing for members of the D.W.U.: whether they were on the left or right. On which side, I wondered, was Mr. Abbott?

The next day there was a high wind, and the waves curled in onto the empty beach, with an anger that seemed out of place in the lost gentility of the pier and its surrounds. The bandstand was empty, although beside the railing on the promenade I saw heavily muffled figures slumped in deck chairs. They looked like some primitive tribe, left out to die in front of the stern, disturbed surface of the ocean.

Abbott was wearing a suede coat that made him look even more like a travelling salesman than ever. He shook me by the hand, and immediately, started off down the promenade.

'It's very good of you to leave the – '

'Oh nothing on today. Meal breaks and protective clothing. There won't be a journalist in the place.'

I hoped he wasn't going to ask me about the everyday life of a private detective. 'Have you had any interesting cases?' that sort of thing. Or 'How do you get into being a private detective?' 'Oh you read a lot and you imagine you are one. Easy.' The only 'case' I'd had prior to the Stan Peace business – unless you count Venables – was finding an old friend's ex-wife for him. Fortunately Abbott seemed to have no interest in such enticing details.

Something I was discovering about being a private detective was that – when you were one – people tended to tell you things. They also tended to shout inexplicable slogans at you, follow you in cars and try to break your arm. Abbott got straight into the confessional routine.

'Look,' he said, 'I hear the police are treating Stan's death as a case of robbery with violence. No way was it that.'

'No?'

'No.'

He looked out at the sea.

'Look. I've been thinking about our conversation. I would like to help you. But – '

'But what?'

'What you're involved in, Mr. Alexander, is extremely dangerous.'

'Yes?'

'Have you – '

'Have I what?'

'Nothing.'

We stopped and stared together down at the beach below. Yesterday there had been something about him I hadn't liked. I could not have said exactly what it was. Today, I found myself warming to him. Why was that? I looked down at him, his blue eyes watering with the cold. Suddenly, I knew what it was. The man was afraid of something. He wanted to confide some secret to me but was frightened to do so. I was sure of it.

'Look Mr. Abbott,' I said, 'I went to see a guy called Ainsworth. He – '

Abbott rounded on me.

'Ask Ainsworth about the Hansbach business,' he said.

'I'm sorry?'

'You heard about the Hansbach business?'

'Not yet.'

'Biggest scandal to hit the labour movement since the E.T.U. monkeyed with a few ballot boxes back in the fifties.'

'Tell me – '

'Ask him about it,' said Abbott. 'Ask him.'

'He won't see me,' I said. 'He's sworn off me.'

Abbott nodded down at the beach. Far away to our left was a group of three men. As I looked across at them, one of them looked up. I recognised, even from this distance the curious devil's tuft of hair and the oddly regular features of Mr. Harry Ainsworth. He looked up at me steadily, and it was I who broke the contact of our eyes, not he. I looked at Abbott and saw that he too was gazing down at the group of three.

'Watch out for Harry Ainsworth,' he said, and then, with the air of a man who feels he has said too much, hurried off down the promenade, wrapping his suede coat about him. I watched him and, when I thought it was safe to do so, looked down again at Ainsworth. He was still looking up at me, levelly, coolly. He looked as if he was trying to make up his mind about something. I looked back out to sea. The way these people behaved was utterly theatrical and ridiculous, but, like a performance in a theatre, it was done with sufficient conviction and style to have the required effect.

I had to admit it. I was frightened.

If there was a point when the Stan Peace affair became just that, and not just another unexplainable interlude in a life already famous for its lack of cohesion, I think it was the day I met Paul Tucker. I had followed Abbott to Eastbourne, not because I was determined to find out who killed Stanley Peace, but because I thought he might provide me with a clear and simple explanation for the extraordinary chain of circumstances that seemed to have developed as a direct result of that night on the Wearing Estate. All I wanted was a reason why every single person I talked to in any way connected with the late Mr. Peace was carrying on like the villagers in the vicinity of Castle Dracula.

And all I got was more of the same.

When I left Eastbourne later that morning I was determined to go and do something sensible. If I hadn't run out of petrol I would never have flagged down the first car to pass me on the London Road.

The car was an ancient Morris Minor. Someone had added a new set of wheels to it, and painted it bright mauve. Someone, presumably the same person, had inserted a large sign in the front window that read ROOTS ROCKERS A GO GO. I could not believe, however, that either of these things had been done by the gentleman at the wheel. It was the same mustachioed type who had passed me the list of delegates at the conference on the previous day. Next to him was a man in his early thirties in a white mac. He had thin, weaselly features and the expression of one who has just been summoned away from a particularly successful honeymoon. As the car screeched to a halt, his face crumpled in pain.

'HEADACHE CRISIS DEEPENS IN BRAKE SHOCK HORROR,' he said, in a slow, quiet, pained voice.

'Hop in,' said the man with the moustache. 'Broken down?'

'All I need is a phone,' I said.

The moustache drove in what I can only describe as an 'interested' fashion. He seemed 'interested' to note that when he went round blind corners at nearly sixty miles an hour the vehicle lifted up off the surface of the road on to two wheels. He seemed 'interested', though not especially so, to observe that sudden, violent braking caused the machine to make a noise like a power saw, and when overtaking, particularly on stretches of road in which it was difficult or impossible to see what might lie ahead, a dreamy, almost yearning expression suffered his big, imposing face.

'We too need a phone,' he said.

'CALL GIRLS UNMASKED IN LATE NIGHT UNION DISASTER,' said the white mac.

'My colleague,' said the moustache, 'works for one of the more popular newspapers.'

We were just coming out of the city boundaries when he jerked the wheel hard over to the left and drove off up a road that led back towards the Downs. At first there were rows of semi-suburban houses but then we came into open country, thick hedges and improbably neat fields garnished with improbably clean cows. He seemed to know where he was going. He gave no sign that we had met at the conference, until I said,

'How's the Distributive Workers' Union?'

He gave me a swift, sideways glance.

'Are you local radio?' he said.

'That's right,' I said, feeling vaguely insulted. Wasn't I a bit *old* to be in local radio?

'JOURNALIST IN PUBLIC HOUSE DELAY HORROR' said the white mac. 'MANY DIE.'

The moustache gave the wheel a demented twitch. We leaped into the air and, like some automated cat, landed in the forecourt of a pub called THE SUSSEX YEOMAN. There were quite a lot of Sussex yeomen inside, jangling their car keys and talking about VAT in loud braying voices. The yeomen's wives, in trouser suits and not quite realistic hairstyles, were drinking gins and tonics and laughing at the yeomen's jokes. All of them, yeomen and yeowomen, looked as if they might turn nasty at any moment.

'My name's Paul Tucker,' said the moustache.

'Paul,' said the white mac, 'is to my mind the best of any of us in the group.'

I asked him which group.

'The industrial group,' he said.

Paul Tucker was buying drinks.

'Do you have', he was saying to the barman, 'Wadworth's 6x on gravity flow?'

'TUCKER FLOORS HOME COUNTIES BEER SNOBS,' said the white mac.

When, after a brief, tangy conversation with the barman and two or three of the yeomen, Mr. Tucker returned, he was in the mood to ask me questions. His manner, at first sight orotund and facetious, concealed a professional sharpness that I found unnerving. He wanted to know how long I had worked in local radio, what I thought of the D.W.U., where I intended to work next.

I gave, at first, what I thought were convincing answers to these questions, but after a while became aware that I had better tell Mr. Tucker at least some part of the truth. I didn't tell him anything about what I did, simply gave him an account of my involvement in the Peace affair. He seemed to enjoy this. When I'd finished he said,

'And what do you do for a living exactly?'

I breathed deeply.

'Well,' I said, 'I *used* to be a journalist. Not for local radio though. Odd bits for film companies. Research sort of thing. Then I started to do things for people I knew.'

'What sort of things?'

'Find things for them. Like lost dogs and – '

'Wives?' said white mac.

'That sort of thing.'

Mr. Tucker looked at me wonderingly.

'You're a private detective,' he said.

'Well I wouldn't say that exactly, I – '

He grinned.

'Flaunt it,' he said, 'flaunt it.'

'O.K.,' I said.

I took out a cigarette and lit it. I inhaled deeply. Then I eased my shoulders forward across the table. I looked slowly at Mr. Tucker and then at his friend. They seemed to enjoy this as well.

'That's more like it,' said Mr. Tucker.

Neither of them had heard of Stan Peace. They seemed surprised to learn that Harry Ainsworth had been a friend of his. Ainsworth, Tucker told me, spent most of his time at the Newlands car company. As he talked about it I seemed to remember headlines about the place, but, at first, I thought they must have been suggested by the man in the white mac, since they seemed to bear no relation to the oddly old-fashioned man with the devil's hairstyle and the quaintly conventional features.

'NO GO BROTHER AINSWORTH. WE WANT TO WORK.'

'I can't understand why Harry should behave like that,' said Tucker. 'He is the mildest of men.'

'He is also,' said the white mac, 'a member of the Communist Party.'

'Some of the nicest people I know are members of the Communist Party,' said Tucker.

'Practically all the people you know are members of the Communist Party,' said his companion.

'Sssh,' said Tucker.

I bought the second round of drinks. The yeomen had climbed into their Range Rovers and left the pub to us. It was a pleasant change to be talking to someone who did not confine himself to weird, allusive remarks. Tucker had the journalist's bemused reverence for facts, and as I talked to him I felt some of the excitement of discovery. He had a natural narrative gift, and his voice, easy and florid as his countenance, conjured up an organisation that was, suddenly, much more than the meaningless initials of my child's guide or the faceless, corporate charade of the Empire Leisure Halls.

'The D.W.U.,' said Tucker, 'is a fascinating Union. Fascinating. It's the nearest thing in this country to what I would call a Business Union. By which I don't mean that there aren't other unions that don't invest speculatively in the way the D.W.U. does *or* have similar administrative structures. What's different about the D.W.U. is that its original power base, among semi-skilled workers in manufacturing industry, is very untypical for unions involved in that kind of caper. The G.M.W.U., for example, invests quite heavily in the system it is at some level sworn to oppose. The E.T.U. is – '

'What Paul is trying to say,' said the white mac, who had been finally introduced simply as Smith, 'is that the D.W.U. is broke.'

'The D.W.U. is a walking paradox,' said Tucker. 'It has a left Executive and a right-wing membership. Ainsworth –'

'One thing at a time,' I said. 'This is, as you say, fascinating. But one thing at a time. What exactly is Ainsworth up to?'

'Ainsworth', said Tucker, 'is district organiser for the union. He is responsible for the affairs of the Newlands car plant, where the bulk of the D.W.U. members are to be found, alongside the – '

'STATE OWNED CAR GIANT IN STRIKE THREAT HORROR,' interrupted Smith.

'I remember,' I said.

Mr. Smith had a way of putting things clearly and simply that I liked. If I bother to read a newspaper I read the *Mirror*.

'Ainsworth is the man in the firing line. His members are facing massive redundancies up at Newlands. The executive want him to win a strike vote on the issue, as do the stewards at Newlands.'

I let all the political stuff wash over me. I was looking for something that might explain how Stan Peace came to be on the floor of that flat with the side of his head cratered like a candle. Whatever it was, I was becoming certain, it had something to do with the D.W.U. While Tucker talked I considered the possibility that Peace's death was somehow linked with the high politics of the union. It didn't seem likely. Peace had been no-one of any significance, an unimportant shop steward who just happened to know a man of some influence, i.e. Ainsworth. What was the connection there?

'I wonder', I said out loud, 'whether Stan Peace was in the Party.'

'This is your friend who had his head bashed in?' said Tucker.

'That's it.'

'The British Communist Party', said Tucker, 'is not the beast it once was. It no longer recruits Oxbridge chaps for Moscow. All that's over. It winges on about things like unemployment and – '

I let him talk again. Something was worrying me. It wasn't until Smith had risen to get in the third round of drinks that I realised what it was. I let Tucker finish anyway, and when he offered to 'show me the ropes' up at Newlands I accepted greedily. Smith returned with the glasses, I waited until we were settled and then, quickly and casually, I said,

'Ever heard of the Hansbach affair?'

Tucker's lips froze over his pint. Then he said, a little too lightly,

'No. Why?'

'Just wondered,' I said.

I saw Smith looking at him.

'Paul would tell me if he had. Wouldn't you Paul?' he said.

'Trust', said Tucker sonorously, 'is essential between journalists. Even when they work for different branches of the capitalist Press.'

'You *have* fucking heard of it,' said Smith. And he looked at me accusingly.

'What is it?' he said; there was a slightly petulant tone to his voice. Information, whether you're a journalist, a detective, or somewhere between the two, is the most important commodity in life.

'I don't know,' I said. 'That's why I asked.'

Tucker gave me a long stare. We finished our drinks, I thanked the two of them and we agreed to meet up at the Newlands factory the following week. At least it might be a chance of getting a little closer to the mysterious Mr. Ainsworth. Anyway, in due course, there were some questions I wanted to ask Mr. Tucker. If he had never heard of Stanley Peace, how did he know that he had been killed by a blow or blows to the side of the head? I may be a thirty-eight year old failure who drinks too much, but I do have fairly good recall of my immediate conversation. I hadn't said anything about *how* the man was killed. I had simply said that he was dead when I found him.

In the car all the way up the A22 I thought about Susan. I thought about her and Saul. I thought about them in bed and her saying things like 'You love me so well' and 'Yes yes yes it's good' and all the things she used to say to me –

greatly to my embarrassment – when we were making love. Saul would love them though wouldn't he? 'Yes I do love you so well,' I could hear him murmur, 'I come into your extensive gardens at rear. Oh that through lounge . . . '.

I had to face the fact. Susan was a woman of no taste whatsoever. I should have known as much when she picked me up off the floor of a party given by a man called Trumpington-Smythe. I didn't need Susan. I was a private eye wasn't I? If the published literature was anything to go by, very soon I was going to meet an attractive, hard-eyed blonde who would go to bed with me before revealing that she was the murderer.

'I'm turning you in sister,' I said, as I veered left on to the M25. 'I'm afraid you're going to have to go over for it.'

The trouble was, there didn't seem to be any women involved in the Peace affair. Trades unions seemed to consist almost entirely of men in suits.

And then I remembered something Dave Abbott had said:

'Did Ella hire you?'

Stan Peace had had a wife. Why didn't I go and see the wife?

Like most ideas that start as a joke, I ended up taking this one seriously. If Ella was the kind of woman who did hire private detectives, well, perhaps it was she who had read my ad in the *Wandsworth News*. She would certainly be one of the first people I had ever met who *did* hire private detectives, which explained why I was driving a ten-year-old Cortina with a faulty fuel gauge.

'Ella,' I said to the dashboard, 'you're going to have to go over for it.'

'Don't honey,' she said.

I had a clear picture of Ella. She had blonde hair and a delicate profile and wore a black cocktail dress even at ten in the morning. Then, as the afternoon grew dark and I came up into Kingston, I realised that she was probably a woman of fifty with three kids and the sort of puzzled face you see in bus queues. This, after all, was England, poor under-nourished England, where even crime doesn't pay a living wage and where we leave law enforcement to the police. Suckers that we are.

When I got back to the flat, Maggie was in the front garden in a kind of red tulle shroud. She was doing an Isadora Duncan style dance.

'Are you O.K.?' I said.

'Bit pissed,' she said.

It was only then I saw she was carrying a trowel. She did not yet seem to have got round to digging anything with it, which relieved me somewhat.

'What are you doing?' she said, when I had manoeuvred her inside.

'Nothing serious,' I said. 'A man got killed that's all.'

'Oh Charlie,' she said, 'you are marvellous.'

'Yeah,' I said.

The next day I went to see Ella Peace. It was strange going back to the flat. I went up by the outside stairs, and waited for quite a long time before going onto the landing where I had heard the noise only two or three nights ago. I expected, somehow, that there would be some trace of what had happened. Chalk marks in the corridor perhaps, or a smear of blood on the door that, as I faced it, brought back the absurd horror of that night, the stagey croaks of the dying man and the blood that was real and would not go away. As I banged on the door – there did not appear to be a bell – I thought about the night my father had died in that hospital outside Paris.

'Jesus,' Susan had said, 'this is just like those films. You know? When people die in films. It's just like this.'

'Yes,' I said, 'they go to a lot of trouble to make it real.'

The door was not opened by a woman in a black cocktail dress, however, but by a boy of about seven, marked with too much adult knowledge and too much adult pain for my middle-class sensibility to enjoy. I like children like Ben – vain, innocent, childlike children. Children who have no idea what's going to hit them. This one had a very good idea. In fact, to judge from the way he opened the door and the cautious glance he gave me, most of it had already hit him.

'Your Mum in?' I said.

'You Council?' he said.

'No.'

'Not the Law are you?'

'I'm a friend of your Dad's.'

Somewhere at the back of the eyes, a light went on, briefly. I had a momentary picture of Stan Peace walking this kid along some canal, his hand on his shoulder, of the boy and him kicking a football across that patch of waste ground the other side of the estate. Was Stan Peace that kind of father? I certainly wasn't. Perhaps that was why I was plagued with this wildly sentimental picture of others' lives? Perhaps that was why I was standing, unpaid, on the doorstep of a stranger. Because I didn't understand myself I was doomed to be here trying to understand others.

'She's in the launderette,' he said, 'bottom of this block.'

'Thanks,' I said.

The launderette was in a row of shops just opposite the block where I had found Stan Peace's body. The shops looked as if they were prepared for some form of civil war – heavy metal grilles, bleak, forbidding notices, and, in one, a wooden board instead of the usual glass pane. Maybe that was the product of the riots, although the two or three dispirited black youths, leaning against the far wall, did not look as if they would be able to summon the enthusiasm necessary for a real riot.

I was prepared for any kind of woman, of course, except the one I found. She was at the far end of the launderette, pulling clothes out of a machine. She had a thin, pale face, but the features were not what you noticed about it. What you noticed were the eyes. The woman's personality – though that was a feeble word for what I saw there – was touchingly, helplessly present in them. It was as if, in the merest glance, she could not help but confide her most intimate secrets. That pure presence of herself – if I didn't think *that* was a hopeless word as well I would call it her soul – that awful vulnerability, shocked me into a silence I had not intended, so that I found myself gawping at Ella Peace, like a tourist before some often seen, barely comprehended monument. She looked at me sharply.

'Woss up wiv' you?'

She had another woman's voice. Or maybe she *was* that other woman and had stolen someone else's eyes. The voice shocked me into further silence.

'No more service washes love.'

'I hadn't – '

She put her head to one side, as she began to fold a blanket. There was suddenly something coquettish about her. I wasn't sure I liked this.

'You're Ella Peace.'

'So?'

'It's about Stan Peace. I – '

I certainly wasn't prepared for what came next. Mrs. Peace yanked out a soggy length of blanket from the machine and hurled it at me with furious accuracy and venom. This was only the beginning. She followed it with a tea towel, a clump of shirts and underclothes and finally the plastic basket she had at her feet. All the time she was screaming senseless, high-pitched obscenities. In the middle of her rush of words I made out ' . . . all the fucking same coming down here I *know* all the fucking same don't try to tell me he doesn't know anything I don't know anything I can't tell the difference between you foreign bastards you . . . '.

Then she stopped, suddenly. For the first time she took in my appearance, the once elegant suit, the heavy shoes. Or maybe it was my voice. I try to alter my accent to suit the furniture – it often seems the politest thing to do – but there's something about the middle-class voice that can't be smothered. She stood in silence for a moment, and when she spoke again her voice was quiet and low. I was no more than a yard from her. The high comedy of her original attack had evaporated. Now I could smell the drink on her breath. There was something tragic and ugly about her as she said –

'Did He send you?'

She pronounced the capital H with a little swagger of sarcasm. I had the impression of someone who thought He was a bit of all right. And yet, hard on the heels of the contempt, as if He (whoever He might be) was listening to her blasphemy and had ways of punishing her for her errors, came the screaming again, a wild desperate noise, as if she was trying to drown the noise of her own fear.

'TELL HIM HE CAN FUCKING WELL COME DOWN HERE HIMSELF NOT SEND HIS FUCKING MINIONS YOU TELL HIM TO COME HIMSELF MY CHRIST WHAT THE FUCK DO YOU THINK I AM I CAN ONLY STAND SO MUCH TELL HIM TELL HIM THAT TELL THE BIG FUCKING BOSS THAT YOU LITTLE SUCK CANCHER?'

I was backing out of the door now. She came after me, still screaming. Even when I was out in the street she followed me, that wild unearthly voice rising and rising, trumping its own hysteria.

'TELL 'IM THAT CANCHER EH? TELL 'IM THAT . . . '

When she turned to go back and I went towards the car, I saw a tiny little girl, of about six, had been watching us.

Slightly self-consciously, I grinned at her. She did not grin back.

'Pissed again,' she said.

'That's it,' I said.

When I got back to the car, three or four teenage lads were trying to take it to pieces. They let me get in it, but did not actually stop what they were doing until I had started the engine. As I drove back towards Putney, I felt as if I were leaving a war zone.

Maybe Stan Peace had a sister. Maybe *she* wore a black cocktail dress.

If your wife ever leaves you – move. Don't stay in your old house. She'll want to come back for the toaster and the dishwasher and all those silly little things women seem to like so much. If you move out of the family home, get somewhere a long way away. Because, even if she left you and you were completely faithful, remember it's All Your Fault. And every time you meet she will remind you of that fact.

Saul and Susan were staying in Saul's luxury home facing the river. 'Five bedroomed Georgian mansion furnished in highly contemporary style with loft area cum playspace. Owner is estate agent so decorated throughout to the point of physical nausea.' I was only three streets away. So we kept meeting, those first few weeks after she left.

She'd met Saul through a house, and houses seemed to be their chief point of communication. I could imagine them in the evenings sitting by the open plan thru sinkunit cum television room cum playspace cum loft/eating area, and leafing through the catalogues Susan was always trying to get me to buy.

'Sorry love,' I'd say, 'but it's not on for a private detective to live in a three bedroomed house. It's all wrong for the image.'

'You are not', she'd say, 'a private detective. Private detectives are grubby little men who chase after divorces, or used to. Actually I don't think there *are* any private detectives any more.'

Oh yes there are. There's me for a start. I'm the last one left in Britain. I know I am.

The first time I met her after she'd left me I was buying a chop in the butcher's. A man in front of me was buying two chickens, three pounds of steak, two pheasants and a capon. I was buying – or planning to buy – a small lamb chop, New Zealand for preference. On that occasion we avoided each other's eyes. On the second occasion, however, Ben made it necessary for us to talk. Largely because, a couple of days after I had seen Ella Peace for the first time, when I was standing at the bend in the river, just below the White Hart, reading a letter from a Japanese businessman who wanted me to get him out of the country by boat on February 12th 1985 (very precise the Japanese), I felt two small arms circle round my waist, and a voice said,

'Got you Charlie.'

I turned round and hugged him. I was going to whirl him round me, the way I used to do, and then, like the self-conscious bastard I am I caught myself thinking 'Oh no. Oh no. Saul does that'. Not that Ben would have been making comparisons. I turned and saw Susan, with Rupert and Toby. Rupert and Toby looked, as usual, fairly implacable. Susan tried to smile.

'Hullo,' I said.

'Hullo,' she said. 'How's business?'

'Business is good,' I said.

I was going to show her the letter but decided against it. Susan's method of showing disapproval of my criminal friends was to pretend they did not exist. She liked to think that the phase of my life when I met them – when I was in the Army – did not happen either. 'Listen,' I used to say to her, 'these things happen. Everyday people get dropped in rivers and fall down on drug deals and want to murder their wives. It's another area of human activity. It needs to be serviced. It fascinates me I'm afraid. It fascinates me.'

'It may happen,' she'd say, 'but not to people like you.'

It was Susan who had wanted to call the firm Information Services. I mean ideally she would have liked me to call it The Times Literary Supplement or the Barnes Footwear Cooperative because, at heart, Susan was a money snob as well as a culture snob.

'Are you doing any pieces?' she said.

She always called them 'pieces'. She thought it was a smart literary way of referring to the half-baked lies used to pad out newspapers. If I ever attempted to call my odd bits of business 'cases' she would give me a kind of pitying smile.

'Here comes Humphrey Bogart,' she'd say.

I looked at her neat black hair, her outdoor complexion and her Burberry raincoat. Already she was beginning to look like an estate agent's wife.

'No,' I said, 'I am not doing any pieces.'

To irritate her, I passed her the letter. She looked at it and sniffed slightly.

'Grow up,' she said.

'Into what?' I said. 'An estate agent?'

'Listen – '

'Oh stuff it,' I said. 'Just because I like villians. I'd rather drink with them than the sort of stupid, snobbish twerp you get mixed up with. Christ, your fucking Saul is a bigger villain than half the – '

'SHUT UP CHARLIE! SHUT UP!'

Ben's mouth had turned down. He looked as if he was going to cry. I remembered a scene at the flat, with me by the window. I had started by shaking her shoulders. I had ended by striking her across the face. Bad form. I looked down at Ben, whose eyes travelled up to mine.

'Don't argue,' he said. 'Please don't argue.'

'I'm sorry,' I said.

Susan too looked abashed.

'Why do we end up hurting each other like this?' she said.

'Because it's something to do.'

'Saul's bought a place in the country.'

'Oh.'

Well it was better than having to meet like this. I wanted to tell her about the Stan Peace affair but couldn't find a way of doing it. In the end I said,

'Have you ever heard of the Hansbach affair?'

'Why do you ask?'

But once again I could see that practical mind turning the question over. I looked down at Rupert and Toby. Toby gave me one of his shy, overwhelming smiles. The stupidity and pointlessness of my life struck me forcefully. Susan finished paging her own brain and said,

'What's it to do with?'

'Some political scandal maybe . . . '

'I'll ask Saul,' she said.

I turned away again. She called after me and so did the children but I didn't turn back. Childish behaviour I know. I'm a grown man. I ought to be able to control my feelings, to make everyone else feel good and then retire to the lavatory to sob my heart out. Ben ran after me in the end, and I turned and kissed him. Being a sloppy middle-class child, he kissed me back. I looked over his head at Susan, her Burberry and her coiffure, and the image of Ella Peace came to me, clearly and simply. I'll go and see that woman again, I thought, cocktail dress or no cocktail dress.

When they had gone I went into the White Hart and ordered a triple whiskey and a jumbo sausage.

'Rave on,' said the barman.

'I'm going to have a tequila sunrise next,' I said.

'Not here you're not, sunshine,' said the barman.

That afternoon I wrote to the Japanese businessman and said that of course I would get him out of the country on the date specified but I would like to know the precise hour of day at which he wished to leave. I thought that would impress him. Then I played poker with Maggie. The next morning (or maybe the morning after that) I went up to Newlands to check up on Mr. Ainsworth.

I was due to meet Tucker and Smith at Gate Fifteen. The

Newlands factory – I read in my newspaper that very morning – was 'trouble wracked'. Well one of the key problems facing its empire was clearly the difficulty of getting into the place. Finding Gate Fifteen took me about half an hour, by which time Tucker and Smith had disappeared. About fifty yards away, on the other side of the yard, I could see a crowd gathered, and, beyond it, on what looked like a scaffold, I saw the figure of Harry Ainsworth. He was shouting something through a microphone. A fat man in a car coat approached me.

'Ted Chabot *Standard*,' he said. 'Have they taken it?'

'Charlie Alexander Local Radio,' I said. 'I don't know.'

'5 to 1 they don't come out,' said the man.

'Yes?'

'Ainsworth doesn't want them to either.'

I listened to some of the speech. As far as I could tell, from this distance, Mr. Ainsworth seemed to be asking his members to come out on strike. I suggested to the man in the car coat that this was a curious way of expressing the contrary opinion.

'He's got to *say* that,' said the man, 'but he doesn't want them out. He's got his bloody hand in the till, Ainsworth has. This lot couldn't afford a one-day stoppage in a funeral parlour.'

There was a man on the gate in a donkey jacket, but Mr. Chabot waved his card and we were let through.

'Where's your tape recorder?' he said.

'I never use a tape recorder,' I said, knowingly.

He gave me a sideways look. When we got to the edge of the crowd I saw Smith and Tucker. People all around us were raising their hands. Mr. Chabot raised his.

'I always vote on these occasions,' he said. 'I think unions should be run democratically. Everyone should participate.'

Mr. Chabot voted for both of the motions, neither of

which I could hear, which I considered very democratic of him. I watched Ainsworth, and Paul Tucker watched me. A man up on the platform had decided that we were in favour of strike action. The two men nearest to me seemed to disagree with this. Someone started booing. Ted Chabot shouted 'Resign' and produced a hip flask.

'So what happens to the union now?' I asked.

'It applies for an overdraft,' said Tucker.

'Paul,' I said, 'is there some financial scandal connected with the D.W.U.?'

'There are rumours,' said Tucker. 'There are always rumours.'

It was then that I noticed Ainsworth. The rest of the stewards from the platform were huddled together near one of the microphones, but Mr. Ainsworth was hurrying away from the crowds, over the tarmac yard, towards the huge lorry park that lay on the other side of the factory. It had started to rain. I slipped away from my companions and, keeping Ainsworth in view, began to thread my way through the crowd, streaming in the opposite direction from me.

'Who are you after?' Tucker called.

I turned back to him. He looked rather like an aristocrat down on his luck, standing in the swirl of a workaday crowd. His big, composed features wore an expression of amusement.

'Ainsworth,' I said. 'I'm very suspicious of people in a hurry.'

'Proper little tec aren't we?' said Tucker.

Ted Chabot was writing something in a flat notebook. Smith looked surprisingly drunk for this hour of the morning. He waved at me.

'MAD MILITANTS IN SUICIDE STRIKE BID VOTE FRAUD,' he said.

Ainsworth didn't look like a mad militant. He looked

worried. He went out of one of the far gates, and, to my relief, doubled back along the service road towards a line of cars. I was parked there. He climbed into a small, newish car and groped under the dashboard for something. I ran along the line of cars to mine, and by the time I had pulled out into the road Ainsworth was already disappearing round the corner. I accelerated.

At first I tried staying three cars behind and looking sinister, but this proved difficult as there was hardly any traffic on the road. As we came into Croydon, however, a juggernaut cut in between me and my target, and it was only when Ainsworth pulled off to the left that I saw his car again. I followed him up a side street, saw him stop, accelerated past and, turning in to the next road, parked and retraced my steps. He was getting out of the car, moving almost at a run. I hurried after him. He went back on to the main road, walked about fifty yards and turned into a dingy-looking shop. I waited. After about five minutes he emerged. I didn't follow him this time. Over the door of the shop was a sign that read FRIENDSHIP TOURS. In the window were pamphlets telling you of the joys of a holiday on the Black Sea, large pictures of minarets and girls in peasant costumes and, in pride of place, a gigantic poster that said simply BULGARIA. No need to say anything else. Just say BULGARIA and they'll come running. I went in.

A fat man was making a cup of tea behind the counter.

'Hullo,' I said. 'Can you book me in with Harry Ainsworth?'

He looked at me narrowly.

'Uh?'

'On the Bulgarian trip.'

He put down the battered kettle.

'He's actually just come back,' he said; 'who did you say you were?'

'Special Branch,' I said, 'but *nice* Special Branch.'

I was out of the place before he could throw a copy of the Rumanian railway timetable at me. When I was on the street again I looked back up at the sign above the door. I thought about how Stan Peace was supposed to be a hard line Stalinist. I thought about Mr. Ainsworth's fascination with Bulgaria. Then I remembered the first thing Ella Peace had said to me. Something about being a foreign geezer . . . .

I got in the car and drove back towards Wandsworth.

She was still in the launderette. She looked as if she had been standing in the same position by the machine since I had last left her. Only this time her dyed blonde hair looked neater, she wore no make-up, and, instead of the blue overall she had been wearing last time, she was in a respectable, almost dowdy, skirt and jumper. To my surprise she grinned at me, revealing a set of not very good teeth. I liked the grin. It was lascivious to the point of outrage.

''Ullo,' she said.

'Hullo,' I said.

Then she went on with her work.

'Sorry about the other day,' she said. 'I was a bit pissed.'

'That's O.K.'

'I thought He sent yer. That's what pissed me off.'

'Who's He?'

She grinned.

'Nosey parker.'

'Can I buy you a drink?'

'Wouldn't say no.'

So saying she dropped the clothes on the floor, stepped over them and proceeded, in a somewhat regal way, out into the forecourt. She didn't need asking where she was going. The pub was about a hundred yards away and as soon as the barman saw her come round the door he had a double gin poured and ready. I used to know a bloke like that. He had the same way of drinking too – as if he didn't notice the drink was there. I ordered myself a beer and took her to a table in the corner.

'What are you?' she said.

'I'm a private detective,' I said.

She didn't raise her eyebrows at this, or make smart remarks about Raymond Chandler's early work. She asked me who was paying me.

'No-one,' I said. 'Except that I keep getting this crazy notion that people are trying to kill me. You see, Mrs. Peace, I found your husband's body. It was me who rang the police. My name was in his address book. Someone stole all but the first page off me. I think there was something in that address book that, if I'd seen it, would tell me something I am not supposed to know.'

'Such as?'

I took a drink.

'Maybe he was killed because of something he'd written in that book. A name.'

'Of?'

'I don't know. Some . . . foreigner . . . '

'Such as?'

'Did your husband ever go to Eastern Europe, Mrs. Peace? To Bulgaria, for example?'

Ella threw back her head and laughed.

'Oh dear,' she said, 'you are a private detective, aren'-cher?'

I felt offended.

'Stan was always drinking with that lot,' she said. 'It was Bulgaria this and Bulgaria that with Stan. Couldn't get enough of Bulgaria. No place on earth like Bulgaria according to him. But he'd never bin there. And I can't see Stan being a spy . . .'

She laughed again, loudly. I let her finish, then I said, quickly.

'Who's He?' I voiced the capital, as she had done. Her face closed up.

'Listen,' she said, 'you can buy me a drink. You can talk to me. I happen to like your face. But don't ask me any more questions. I'll be off if you ask any more questions. I might even throw something at yer.'

She laughed again, and this time I joined in. Even if she wouldn't answer questions, I reflected, she was worth talking to. Every time she laughed I got a good look at those evil-looking teeth, and as she tilted her neck back I could see that her breasts were small and full.

'Why don't you let me buy you dinner?' I said.

'The boy'll have to come,' she said.

'Of course,' I said.

'You won't talk about Stan?' she said.

'Of course not,' I said.

We made a date for the following week. When I got up to go, she pulled me down to my seat again. Suddenly her face was desperate.

'Not till they close,' she said, 'please . . . '

'Where's your boy?'

'Asleep.'

I left.

When I got back to the flat there were two messages on the answering machine. The first was from Paul Tucker. He announced that he was going to ACAS next Wednesday morning and would I like to accompany himself and Mr. Smith. They had, he told me 'something to my advantage'. Then Mr. Smith started to sing an Irish traditional melody. Then they were cut off. The second was more interesting. It was from Dave Abbott. Unlike most people who find themselves confronted with an answering machine, Mr.

Abbott adopted a relaxed, casual manner, as if used to the formal etiquette of communication by machine.

'... Look I was being foolish the other day. There are just certain things I don't like to talk about. But what I wanted to make clear is that our friend Mr. Ainsworth is on the board of the Newlands Pension Fund. Handling millions of pounds. And from what I hear that body could use some investigation. Now, you know about pension funds, don't you Mr. Alexander? Give me a ring up at Fairlie's tomorrow. We'll have a talk, O.K.?'

I was in the middle of admiring Mr. Abbott's cosy conversational style, when a brick came through the window, narrowly missing my head. I heard a van out in the street, but before I had time to get out and see who was in it, it had accelerated off down towards the river. The most eerie thing of all was, as it went, I heard a voice screaming something at me. I caught my name and then a few foul words and that was all. Maggie appeared from her front window in a white towelling dressing-gown.

'Darling,' she said, 'are we being mugged?'

'It's O.K.' I said, 'Really.'

It was curious. I'd been expecting something like this to happen. Ever since that evening in the Wearing Estate, I had been unable to rid myself of the feeling that I was being watched. Did someone know how far I had got? And, if so, why should they start warning me off again at this stage of the proceedings? I got out the one sheet of paper I had managed to retain that day at the airfield. Was there a name there that would mean something to me? MARXOFF, IVAN, SPY, TEL: SOFIA 5432.

There was only one name left I hadn't tried:

MO ALLEN.
EXETER FILMS
BROADWICK STREET.

Then the number.

That didn't look particularly significant. What then? Why should whoever it was who was stealing things off me and chucking bricks through my window, choose tonight to start hotting up the proceedings?

Well who had I been following? Who had seen me with Abbott on the promenade at Eastborne? Who, according to Mr. Abbott, was involved in something called a pension fund?

I didn't know anything about pension funds. Being a private detective is not pensionable. In the days when I was even more insecure than I am now about so describing myself I approached an insurance company about what Susan optimistically called my 'future'. I was forced to describe myself accurately for once. The man was at first incredulous then boyishly enthusiastic.

'What do you do?' he said.

'Anything legal,' I said.

'Are you a hit man?'

'No,' I said, feeling somewhat peeved, 'I'm a private detective.'

He was a tiny man in a neat black suit. He leaned over the desk.

'Have you got a gun?'

'Yes,' I said, 'I have. Not *on* me but I have.'

His eyes shone with pleasure.

'I think,' he said, scrabbling in his desk feverishly, 'I've got just the pension plan for you.'

I worked out later it would have cost me my income for the last three years to buy his pension plan. Also I didn't like the idea of people knowing how much I earned. My work tends to be cash, although sometimes, as with the Stan Peace affair, it's a question of trying to avoid being taken apart.

Over the next few days, as well as asking about boats for my Japanese friend, and having a useful drink with a youth named Harry the Dog (who is, in a way, a story all of his own), I found out *all* about pension funds. The woman in the library seemed to approve of the direction my reading had taken. I rang an old friend in Fleet Street and got hold of a cuttings file, which proved, to my satisfaction, something I had always suspected – the larger and more apparently respectable a financial institution, the dodgier it is.

A company like Newlands had a pension fund of literally millions. All over the country, it appeared, wage slaves were paying large chunks of their salary into special accounts, which were then, supposedly, invested by the big-wigs, so that, one day, the said wage slaves, would enjoy a cottage in Devon along with all the other shagged out wage slaves. Sounded fine. In fact of course, as always, half the people who administered these things were either bent themselves or knew someone who was a bit that way. With that amount of money at your disposal, you could make the Stock Exchange move a few points, according to where you shifted the loot. There were, it appeared, bands of criminal sounding persons called investment consultants who spent their lives doing just this. Union representatives, it appeared, were from time to time, to be seen as trustees on the boards responsible for administering all this cash, and presumably, got within smelling, if not touching distance of the kind of money that could . . . .

That could what? Start a Bulgarian fruit farm? Finance a strike? None of this sounded quite good enough. If Ainsworth was up to some fiddle with the Newlands Pension Fund, just how did he swing it? And what did this have to do with hard line Stalinist Stan Peace?

I went to sleep on Tuesday night and dreamed that Ella

Peace and I were having dinner with Mr. Ainsworth on a yacht in Bulgaria. Then the police arrived and took Ainsworth – who now had Abbott's face – away in a black van. As the van drove off it started hooting, long and mournful like a steamer in fog. The hooting would not go away, and with a start I realised it was coming from the street below. I looked out of the window and saw a black cab, outside which was Paul Tucker.

'Enter,' he boomed, 'and I will request the non-unionised driver of this vehicle to proceed to the offices of ACAS, where even now the future of the D.W.U.'s strike is being debated at the highest level.'

Tucker had a way of talking to everyone as if they were a copy taker. I was waiting for him to say 'full point new par open quotes Caps The Strike Torn Firm . . . ' but before he could do anything of the kind Smith's head came out of the cab window.

'AINSWORTH IN PEACE BID WITH HARRIS FIASCO.'

'I'll be right down.'

If I was going to understand this business I was going to have to understand the affairs of the D.W.U. Simply because they seemed to loom so large for Stanley Peace. As I dressed I rehearsed my current state of knowledge, augmented from a glance at a cuttings file, courtesy of my Fleet Street chum.

The D.W.U. represented semi-skilled workers at the plant and was under pressure from the other two unions involved. It was also under pressure from the management, since, as far as I could gather, the vast majority of the redundancies up at the plant involved D.W.U. members. They had been forced into strike action, since that was the only way to demonstrate the union's strength, and yet, precisely because they represented workers who were not immediately essential to the firm, their strike was doomed. The paradox of trades unions – it was beginning to appear to me – was that, like capitalist firms, only the largest, toughest and most commercially viable survived.

Well, if Ainsworth and his friend, the left-wing General Secretary, didn't make a deal, maybe that would send Ainsworth running for his secret supply of Pension Fund Loot. Or Bulgarian gold perhaps (make a change from Moscow gold). Maybe all this was depressingly thin.

When I got into the cab I noticed that Smith was carving a lemon with fastidious neatness on to a bound copy of the *Times World Atlas*. Next to him on the seat was a bottle of gin and two bottles of tonic. Next to the tonic I noticed a small plastic ice bucket. He poured out three generous doubles and then tapped on the glass.

'Not for me thanks,' said the driver. 'I'm driving.'

Gin and tonic is quite a good breakfast drink. The back of a taxi is usually the sort of place that smells as if you had just put your head into a chamois leather bag. After two large gins, it seemed a much more pleasant place to be.

'Could I be an Industrial Correspondent?' I said.

'You have the stamina,' said Tucker.

'He could have Merrison's job,' said Smith. 'We don't like Merrison. Merrison's a Tory.'

I looked at the two of them. I wanted to ask Tucker straight out about how he had the details of Peace's death. I hadn't seen any reports of it in national newspapers, which figured, if, as Abbott had said, they were treating it as robbery with violence. Nobody is interested in robbery with violence. It is the sort of thing that happens to you and me, isn't it?

They were certainly political people these two. And yet I had the impression that, unlike men like Ainsworth, they were able to play at it. If Tucker was compromised in some way, then it was possible that he was not so compromised that he couldn't talk. After all, Tucker's interest, like mine, was liable to be Information wasn't it? He saw me looking at him.

'You're a calculating little bastard aren't you?' he said in a not unfriendly way.

'I'm a calculating big bastard,' I said.

Smith raised his glass to a passing police car.

'IT'S GIN IN THE FAST LANE: OFFICIAL,' he said, then lay back on the seat. It was impossible to state Smith's age. All you could say with any certainty was that he was languid. He was, I thought, about the most languid person I had ever met in my life.

'I don't know why I said that about Merrison,' he said. 'Merrison's a nice bloke. And he isn't a Tory. He's a paid up member of the Socialist Workers' Party.'

Then, to my immense surprise, he fell fast asleep.

When we got to ACAS Tucker left him in the taxi and strode off towards the little group of photographers and reporters crowding around the entrance to the building. I saw the red-faced man I'd seen at the conference in Eastbourne, Owen Harris, and, behind him, Ainsworth.

'The Management and I', whispered Tucker, 'have had useful talks and I and the other members of the Executive are confident we will see an early end to this dispute.'

I pushed closer to the crowd.

'The Management and I', Mr. Owen Harris was saying, 'have had very useful talks and I and the other members of the Executive feel positive that there will be now a speedy end to this dispute.'

'He's being very volatile today,' said Tucker.

I noticed him make a series of gestures to Ainsworth – rather like a tick-tack man on a racecourse – as the two union men got into the car.

'What did that mean?' I said.

'It meant,' said Tucker, 'see you in the Green Man,

Isleworth, at nine-thirty tonight.'

'How do you know he'll come?'

'By the look in his eye dear boy.'

'Why Isleworth?'

'He lives there.'

Tucker was clearly amused by me. Perhaps, too, he was gratified by this chance to demonstrate his professional skills. Anyway, for some reason of his own he had clearly decided to grant me some of his precious information, and I, with the spirit of the true enquirer, was grateful.

'Look,' he said, 'if you want to know how I know Stan Peace died. Harry Ainsworth told me. Harry happens to be a friend of mine. I like him a great deal.'

Well, I thought, well well well Mr. Tucker, don't let that moustache fool anyone. *You* are not stupid. You ought to be a private detective. He smiled at me wryly and then said,

'And Hansbach is not an East German spy. He's a stockbroker. Go and see him. Here's his address.'

'Thanks Paul,' I said.

'It's a pleasure,' he said, 'I think you're being pointed in the wrong direction.'

When we got back to the taxi Smith was awake.

'COMMUNIST UNION MEN GIVE INTREPID REPORTER SLIP IN SLEEP SHOCK HORROR,' he said.

I nearly ran for the tube station. In my right hand was the address Paul Tucker had given me. In my head was a searching list of questions about pension funds.

The City of London has always amused me. The pomposity of the buildings, the proliferation of solid architecture, all of it somehow designed to conceal the fact that inside these banks and counting houses, all conceived on an Imperial scale, are thousands of clerks with their hands on what brings all this to life, what it lives by and for – thousands and thousands of tiny pieces of paper that have, the best of economists will tell you, only a notional meaning.

Mr. Hansbach lived in the top floor of a modern equivalent of the Temple of Commerce, a twenty or thirty storey building, with a lift that made you feel you had been strapped to a stomach pump and a foyer that had been designed to make the act of waiting seem of cosmic significance.

He was surprisingly easy to get to see. I found that suspicious. I told the man on the desk I was from the *Sunday Times* and engaged in writing a piece about the Newlands car company. Mr. Hansbach would see me straight away. It was funny; in my days as a journalist I had frequently pretended to myself, to get through dull afternoons, that I was a private detective. Now I seemed to be spending my time posing as a journalist.

Mr. Hansbach had the profile of a pterodactyl and the hands of a surgeon. He also, while we're at it, had the suit of an oil millioniare and the expression of a fried fish. He sat behind his desk with his fingertips together. He looked like a man doing an impression of a nineteenth-century diplomat. His act was not helped by his German accent, which was the kind of thing I was used to hearing on the lips of Nazi officers in fifties war films.

'Fot cen I do for you?' he said.

Expecting him at any moment to press a button that would send me straight down to the foyer without benefit of lift, I told him I worked for the *Sunday Times*. He did not ask my name or how long I'd worked there or what the view was when you got out of the lift on the fourth floor. Instead he continued to put his fingertips together and look like a prune.

'Vy hef you gum to zee me ziss day?' he said.

'I'm doing a piece on Harry Ainsworth,' I said, 'a sort of profile. Union man in the firing line sort of thing.'

Mr. Hansbach gave me a smile as thin as the creases on his jacket.

'Herry Ainswurf', he said, as if proud of this information, 'iss a Gommunist.'

'That's right,' I said.

'Ant I', he went on, 'am a stockbroker.'

'Yes,' I said.

He smiled again. I wondered if he smiled at his wife like that, and if so, why she bothered.

'Bud he iss a purrzonal frent a' mine,' he went on. 'Even a Gommunist state needs gut vinancial advice.'

A strange noise, like that of a waste disposal unit, came from deep within Mr. Hansbach's reptilian throat. With a thrill of horror I realised he was laughing. I laughed right along with him. Pretty soon the two of us were chuckling away like hysterical dinosaurs in his circular office, high above the river. When we'd both stopped, I said, quickly,

'I want to know about the Newlands Pension Fund.

His throat started to quiver. A moment later his mouth shut like a trap. He stopped making the noise. When he spoke again his accent had lost some of its theatricality. It was suddenly, almost openly malicious.

'Then why don't you try the *Financial Times* Library?' he said. 'I hear they're very good.'.

When Mr. Hansbach wanted you to leave his office he did not summon heavily armed men. He just looked at you speculatively, as if wondering what you might taste like for lunch, and pretty soon you rose like a glider on a thermal saying things like 'Well well well is that *really* the time?' or 'My my but this *has* been fun . . . ', all the time feeling your throat to make sure it hasn't been sliced through when you weren't looking.

When I got to the door, he said,

'You didn't say your name,' he said.

'Benson,' I said, worried in case he might find out where I lived.

He nodded.

'Goodbye,' he said.

I found the encounter more chilling in retrospect than I had at the time. I set off through the City, trying out a theory that looked a lot better than any I had had so far. I wondered whether it would sound any better if I had an assistant to confide it to. Ainsworth and Hansbach were up to some fiddle with the Newlands Pension Fund. There were any amount of those. Tipping shares, maybe placing D.W.U. investment money in companies bolstered by the Pension Fund millions. Suppose Ainsworth had rumbled the fiddle, and for some devious political reason of his own, cut himself in on it? That theory put together the union's financial crisis, Ainsworth's odd behaviour (if Abbott had rumbled him, he was presumably The Bastard of Fairlie's) and assuming Ainsworth was involved for more than simply financial gain – the weird foreign element mentioned by Ella Peace.

There were some things it didn't explain though. If Mr. Abbott had hard evidence of the fiddle, why hadn't I seen it? Why was Tucker – who, in spite of everything, I had decided was straight – so solidly behind Ainsworth? And who – while we were at it – was He?

I decided to take these problems over towards Fleet Street. I needed a drink. I looked carefully over my shoulder one or two times as I walked. If I was getting close, then whoever had wanted that address book might start to use something more definite than a brick through my window.

Tucker was at his desk in the offices of his newspaper. It was a small desk for a man I was beginning to think of as important. The office was the size of an aircraft hangar. Men in shirtsleeves were studying teleprinters, making telephone calls, holding the front page, while other men behind glass panels at the far end of the room were waving their arms with the slow formality of business conference.

'Let's get a drink,' I said.

'Quite,' said Tucker.

As we walked out into Fleet Street, I told him about Hansbach. He was amused at first, and then, as I had been, more serious. He let me talk, I notice. Whatever he knew about this affair, he was not yet prepared to tell me. I talked to him about Dave Abbott.

'I know him,' was all he said.

We turned off Fleet Street down one of the narrow lanes that lead to the Embankment. It was blocked with gigantic lorries, unloading newsprint. Tucker took my arm and steered me into the next street on the left. I saw the car as soon as we turned the corner. They must have been waiting for us – presumably my companion was always to be found heading for this pub around opening time – for, as soon as they saw us, they drove straight at us, headlights full on. I dived to the left, in the grip of reflexes an Army instructor had once described as 'above average'. But Tucker wasn't so lucky.

The car hit him straight on. He flew up into the air with the speed and ease of a helium balloon ripped out of a child's hand. He hit the pavement with a monstrous, percussive crack. I ran across to him, as the car veered off to the right, down towards the river. There was blood on his face and he seemed to be having difficulty breathing.

'Hansbach – ' he began.

'What about Hansbach?' I said.

I too had watched Francis Durbridge serials. I knew that when seriously wounded people start telling you things you had better listen. I had read Dickens' novels too and I knew that when people look as if they are dying, it is often easy to assume they are speaking the truth. But Tucker didn't say any more about Hansbach or anyone else for that matter. He closed his eyes and lay back on the pavement as if it were a hospital bed.

I'm one of those people who can't stop thinking. Even as I ran back for a telephone, I was thinking 'All right. Hansbach and Ainsworth are up to something. But why should they want Stan Peace topped? Wasn't he a friend of Ainsworth's? Don't they appear to have the same political views?' I was thinking all of this quite urgently, because I was aware that coming up with answers in this case wasn't a matter of salving my professional pride. It was a matter of prolonging my life.

Paul Tucker was lucky. He wasn't dead. He wasn't alive either mind. They took him to hospital in a coma. I went with him in the van. A policeman came and took a statement from me. We both agreed that hit and run drivers ought to be shot. I hung around the ward for a while and discovered Tucker had a wife and three children in Aylesbury. Then I left for the flat. I took the tube. I got into the most crowded carriage I could see and jammed myself up against the doors between stops. When I got to Hammersmith I ran out to the taxi rank and practically threw myself into the back of a cab. It was a bitterly cold night and the forlorn lights of the Hammersmith roundabout slipped away to my left like the lights of the shore seen from a ship that travels towards darkness. When I got back to the flat I double-bolted the front door, and, after I'd left the light in the hall burning, had gone upstairs to bed. I undressed in the dark, lit a cigarette and wished I could get rid of that prickle at the back of the neck. They wouldn't be watching me now. Surely.

In the darkness I got up and went to the window. In the light from the hall I could see, on the opposite pavement, in the shadows by the big tree opposite, a face I knew. He was staring up at the house with the expression of a man who is prepared to wait all night.

It was Dave Abbott.

PART TWO

The first thing I did next morning was to ring the one remaining number in the address book. It was all I could think of to do. I didn't want to spend the rest of the week lying in bed gibbering. MO ALLEN EXETER FILMS. I took the phone back to bed and dialled the number.

She sounded rather different from the other acquaintances of Mr. Peace I had met. She didn't cry or scream or confess to crimes she had not committed. She seemed surprised to hear of Peace's death, but observed a comprehensible level of mourning. She also had a strong Yorkshire accent, which for some reason prejudiced me in her favour.

'Coom over,' she said, 'I'm always here.'

When I had checked that Abbott had camped in the opposite garden (I half expected to see him cooking bacon and eggs over a primus stove) I got dressed and took myself to Berwick Street.

Exeter Films turned out to be two rooms at the top of a flight of stairs. There was a vegetable market in the street outside and most of it seemed to have found its way up the stairs. I kicked a carrot out of the way and leaned on a bell that read:

RING FOR MO ALLEN. FILM-MAKER

The door was answered by a plump, jolly woman of about fifty. Or sixty. Or perhaps, forty. She was wearing a floral smock and what looked like a ginger wig, but her appearance was redeemed by her smile, which was as welcoming as her voice had been.

'Do you want to watch a film about the Third World?' she said.

I said I didn't but thank you.

'Isn't it awful about Stanley,' she said. 'Was it a woman

did it?'

'Why do you say that?'

'Because he was a lecherous little bastard that's why,' said Mo.

'I don't know,' I said. 'That's what I'm here to find out.'

Without waiting for any further questions she got up and waddled to a shelf on the opposite wall. On it were a row of shabby looking film cans. Their labels said things like SALTLEY GATES or TENANTS GROUP STEPNEY 1973. They did not look as if they had been opened for some time. At the very end of the shelf was a small square box, made of green cardboard. Mo plucked it off and flipped it open. She held up a small circle of celluloid.

'Stan Peace,' she said.

Then she waddled back to the viewing machine and buckled the spool of film into position.

'This is film of him . . . ?' I said.

'That's it,' said Mo.

I felt an absurd sense of elation. I don't know why but the prospect of actually *seeing* that man I had watched die in my arms a week or so ago was almost unbearably exciting. When the film flickered into life I knew why. All I had heard was others' opinions of him. He was a Stalinist, a lecher, a Dad . . . . Now I was going to get the chance to judge for myself.

Except, of course, that no-one judges for himself. The picture, the file, even the physical encounter with a fellow human are always mediated by another. Mo was talking, as on the screen I saw a black and white, jerky impression of Gothic buildings.

'Isn't that Oxford?' I said.

'It is. I was on a course with Stan at Ruskin. In the late fifties. Shop stewards' training course.'

Into the picture came a group of men holding beer mugs. They grinned at the camera. It swayed back and then refocussed. I saw a lawn, a stretch of river, and in the distance a mass of tables and chairs. It seemed to be summer. Mo stopped the machine and pointed to a small man with a moustache in the left of the frame.

'That's Stan.'

He did look like a lecherous little bastard. I looked closer at the picture. Behind Stan was a face I thought I recognised. Or rather it wasn't the face – but the neat tufts of hair either side of the ears that gave him the look of a pantomime devil.

'That's Harry Ainsworth.'

'You know Harry. We all knew Harry. It was him got us to join the bloody Party.'

I looked sideways at her.

'This was before Hungary?'

'I don't know,' said Ms. Allen. 'There was a world before and after those occurrences you know.'

It was curious. Her speech had some of the prim, antique quality of Ainsworth's. Assuming she too was a Communist, where did they both acquire this desperate respectability? The film was moving again and she was looking at it, lost in the flickering world of the past, sucked into the picture before her.

'What else was he?' I said, as the scene changed to a grim looking building outside which the same group were posing with the elaborate larkiness of students. 'Besides a lecher, what else was he?'

'Not much,' said Mo. 'He was always in trouble over women. That was where he met Ella of course.'

'His wife?'

'That's right. He pinched her off some feller. There was a heck of a row about it.'

You always loved him, sweetheart, because you're no good. Finally you killed for him didn't you? But I'm going to have to let you go over for it. I thought of the woman with the extraordinary eyes who had flung her day's work at me the first time I met her. The woman who drank large gins faster than I did. To be capable of murder . . . What kind of person did you have to be to batter a man like that? Strong for a start. Unless she jumped him. Unless she was pissed and crazy like she had been that first time.

'He wasn't one of us, though, the feller he pinched her off. He was some sharpie from the town crowd.'

I lost interest in this angle. What had Peace said to me on the night he died? 'Knew him. Knew him.' The film flickered on. I saw Ainsworth on a boat. Saw Peace grab at whoever was holding the camera. Realised that Mo had been holding the camera. Looked at her ash-coloured face and eyes red with study of that screen and wondered why I was so concerned with who had taken a life. Such a small thing to take really. She had stopped the machine again.

'Now that feller fancied her. He was in the bloody race he was.'

I looked at the man she was pointing out. He was standing at the back of the group, holding a glass up to his face. I had the uncomfortable impression I had seen that face before.

'Could you run the film back?'

She ran the film back to the place where the man's face appeared. It was no good. Like a number or a name, half heard, then stirred into life by some other encounter, the man's identity flickered before me like the film then broke up into anonymity. He had an anonymous face. Could be anyone.

'Look,' I said. 'Was there anyone else on that course with you. Who might remember anything about it?'

'There was Gab,' said Mo. 'Gab Johns. Skip Taylor. Peter Stevens. God knows where they are now.'

'I'm looking for anyone and everyone,' I said, 'for any kind of motive. Until I find one that fits perfectly. A row over a woman is a start isn't it?'

'Bloody good start,' said Mo.

She waddled over to a desk in the corner of the room and took out an enormous address book. All these people kept meticulous records. Why? Was it to aid the Special Branch.

'No,' she said, finally. 'All I can recall is their unions. Gab was Electricians. Skip was a building worker, and Peter . . . Peter was a bloody miner I think.'

'You're very kind Ms. Allen,' I said.

'Don't mention it, young man,' she said. 'It's not often I get a young man in here.'

'What about all those hot-headed radicals?' I said.

'They vote Tory now,' she said. 'If they bother to vote.'

I left her sitting in front of the screen gazing at a frozen image of her past. Out in the street market traders were shouting up their bright, wax polished fruit and veg, gazed at by weary-looking women. I blinked as you do when you come out of a cinema into daylight and realised with a shock how much the real world surprised me. I was in Stan Peace's world, I saw suddenly, possessed by the desire to discover what had animated him, what had killed him, and all this, the street, the market, the gaudy shops, was as unreal as a play.

Well, if it was about the woman in the case I might as well go and see her. I rang the hospital to be told that Tucker was still in a coma, took a taxi back to the flat and drove off towards Wandsworth and the Wearing Estate. I wanted to ask Ella about more than the day she met Stan Peace, though. I wanted to know just how friendly Dave Abbott and Mr. Peace had been. It might give me something to talk about when I next tripped over him kneeling at the keyhole of my front door.

She wasn't in the launderette. Maybe she'd found someone who did more than promise to buy her dinner.

Maybe she'd had the luck to meet a man who actually went through with it. I went up to the flat. There was no answer there. I hammered on the door as loudly as I could, and eventually, the door of the flat opposite opened. A cautious faced peered out.

'She's off out of it mate.'

'Where to?'

'Search me. There was the lot here. Social worker. Police . . . . '

He didn't look sorry to have lost Mrs. Peace as a neighbour.

One of the things I always prided myself on was my objectivity. I was usually good at knowing when I was working and when I was not. When I was calculating the chances and strengths of this or that theory and when I was just – you know – *living* like those people in Berwick Street Market. The answer was this simple usually: I was always working. I was never just living. If I made a mistake in the Stan Peace business, it wasn't getting involved with Ella Peace. It was allowing the affair to distract me.

It wasn't hard to find her. I went into the Social Services Department. I didn't stop at Reception. Never stop at Reception. Reception is a waste of time. I went straight up the stairs with the air of a man who has the cares of each and every homeless unmarried immigrant mother in South London on his mind. I didn't just look like a social worker. I looked like a *senior* social worker. When I got to the first landing I went into the first office I saw and asked, in a tetchy voice, to know who was doing the care order on the Peace child. I know all about care orders you see – but that's another story.

'Ruth I think,' said the girl.

It didn't take me long to find Ruth. She was a girl in a trouser suit, who really *had* got the cares of every homeless unmarried immigrant for miles around on her not unappealing shoulders. She'd also got them on her face. In spite of the make-up and the swept-back hair I thought she looked older than she needed. It was only when she started to speak that I realised I disliked her intensely.

'We don't give out personal details Mr – '

'Mr. Zombie,' I said, 'Arnold Zombie.'

This got a wintry smile. She went out into the office to a large room. A lot of people were in this room. Mothers with young children, old men with crumpled faces, a heavily pregnant black girl. They looked as if they had been there a long time. Ruth looked as if she knew exactly what she was going to do with every one of them. It would take her time, but pretty soon there wouldn't be any misery or gloom in the entire borough. Ruth would see to that. She'd split off the Mums from the Dads and the sisters from the brothers and in no time everyone would have just the one Mum Dad Sister and Brother rolled into one. Superwoman in a trouser suit.

'You think you're absolutely fucking wonderful don't you?' I screamed, as Ruth strode purposefully towards the waiting crowd, file in hand. Social workers think they're God-all-bleeding-mighty. I was married to a woman like you once she thought she was God-all-bleeding-mighty she –'

That's what I mean about getting involved with Ella. Oh I was doing all this for effect. I was watching myself do it and noting the effect it had on her, which was, as I intended a strong desire to leave the room in case she stopped looking like superwoman and came to resemble one of the homeless unmarried immigrant wrecks who were in need of her help. But, as well as *doing* my number, I found myself *feeling* it.

I was put in care you see, when I was six. Aaahh . . . .

She retreated to her office and slammed the door behind us.

'Sneer', she said, 'all you like. If you want to know the bloody woman's too pissed most of the time to know where she is and the kid is better off being with someone who can look after him and if you want to know those bed and breakfast places in Leinster Road are luxury as far as I am concerned they – '

She stopped and put her hand to her mouth.

'Leinster Road,' I said. 'Thanks. You're a bit more bearable when you're angry.'

'Who did you say you were?'

'Zombie,' I said, 'Arnold Zombie. *News of the World*.'

She looked as if she was calculating the chances of her holding on to her position of trust and confidence as I left. I figured this would give her new insights into the problems of the insecure and difficult people with whom I was sure she had to deal every day.

Ruth's idea of luxury wasn't mine. Ella Peace's new apartment reminded me of the sort of place favoured by assassins on the run. It combined anonymity with menace. She was sitting on the bed, staring at the dirty net curtains. She wasn't drunk, but she had obviously been crying a lot and those big eyes had invaded the rest of her face. Her shoulders were hunched forward and she did not look up when I entered the room.

'How did you find me?'

I told her. She enjoyed the story.

'I was pissed,' she said, 'and then I hit Tommy.'

I sat on the bed and put my arms round her.

'What do you see in me?' she said, 'I'm old. I'm stupid. I'm ugly.'

'I don't think you're old,' I said.

That made her laugh again. She turned her thin, ravaged face to me and I kissed her lips. They were dry and soft.

'Your place or mine?' I said.

'This,' she said, 'is council property, mate.'

She moved in with me that afternoon. It was funny. Immediately she was in the flat I felt safe. Now I know *why* I felt safe, but the memory has still to do with waking next to her and the way her body felt above or below me on the cold nights that went on for as long as I knew her. She couldn't cook, she couldn't make conversation, she couldn't clean or scrub or calculate or any of the things Susan had been able to do. But still – I liked her fine.

I'd given up on Mr. Ainsworth. I'd rung people I knew but found nothing at all to wrap up these rumours about Pension Fund fiddles. Anyway I had another suspect.

Three or four days after we went to collect Ella's son from the children's home I asked her about Dave Abbott.

'Was Dave a good friend of Stan's?' I said.

'No he bloody wasn't,' she said, and then, as she always did when I had conned her into talking about Peace, pressed her lips together tightly. I let it go. My worry about Abbott was simply that he had the same coy reluctance to amplify his doubts and conclusions as Tucker. If there was a fraud, perhaps it was more complex and compromising than one left union leader and a stockbroker. That seemed a fairly unlikely combination anyway.

The social worker called Ruth came round to check I had hot and cold running water and that I wasn't going to batter little Tommy any more than he had been already. Little Tommy looked on sullenly.

'You should see my wife,' I said. 'Now she really does need a social worker.'

'Oooh does she?' said Ruth eagerly.

'Yes,' I said, 'she's married to an estate agent.'

'It's easy to sneer at people like me,' she said.

'Yes,' I said, 'it is.'

When Ella and her son were settled in I went to see Dave

Abbott with the list of names given to me by Mo Allen. He wasn't at the airfield. I rang the D.W.U. Headquarters and asked after him.

'Oh no,' they said, 'Mr. Abbott's no longer at Fairlie's. Mr. Abbott is a full time official of the union.'

I wondered whether this was promotion. A Smith-like headline flashed through my mind as I drove down to the factory in Kent, where I had been told I would find him. AMBITIOUS UNION MAN MURDERS STEWARD IN PROMOTION ROW. What I couldn't make fit about any of this was the pathetic amounts of money involved, the low stakes. Maybe the row over a woman was a better guess.

Dave Abbott wore the same suit and had the same air of having been recently dry-cleaned while actually wearing it. His eager bulbous eyes looked me up and down as he said,

'I'll do my best to trace these men for you Charlie.'

'Thanks,' I said.

The factory was one of those small engineering concerns that look as if they must be a front for some other activity. I went out through the yard to my car, and, to my surprise, saw none other than Mr. Ainsworth standing by one of the doors. He was carrying a black briefcase. He didn't appear to have seen me. Then I saw Abbott. He came down a flight of steel stairs running close to the side of the building and, again unseen by me, he stopped as soon as he saw Ainsworth. I saw Ainsworth turn round and march towards him. Abbott was still wearing that bland all-purpose smile of his as Ainsworth grabbed him by the lapel. I saw the two of them shout at each other. Abbott tried to wrench the older man's hand from him but Ainsworth hung on. Then they started pushing at each other. Finally they broke, and I saw Abbott hurry off towards the car park.

Then Ainsworth caught sight of me. I waved at him gaily. It was all I could think of to do. He did not wave back. He swung his black briefcase into the air and set off in my direction. I stayed where I was. When he reached me I noticed the tufts of hair by each ear had become slightly disarrayed. He looked, although he did not smell of drink, like a drunken barber.

'Leave me alone you little pillock can't you?' he said.

'If you'll tell me who's chucking bricks through my window, I will,' I said.

Ainsworth snorted.

'How much are they bloody paying you?' he said, and marched off after Abbott.

I didn't attempt to answer him. The answer was too shaming. I drove off back to the flat and my new family. Buy them off the peg. Ready-made wife and son. No problem.

They had started to put Christmas decorations in the shops as I came up through Streatham. Santa Claus and his reindeer grinned out at me from electrical shops. Outside the Pentecostal Church the sign read CUSTARD CHRISTIANS ARE AFRAID OF TRIFLES. I thought about Susan's new house with Saul deep in the country. They would have a tree and an advent calendar and paperchains in the hall and a proper Christmas dinner. Maybe I would take Ella down to see them. And Tommy.

Why did all this public charity make me feel so sour? And why did I feel so safe all of a sudden? Was I falling in love with the damn woman?

BUY HER A RADIO THIS CHRISTMAS, said a sign in a shop. LET HER KNOW YOU CARE.

Saul and Susan were very good about Christmas. It was important Daddy saw the children. When would Daddy like to come? Daddy could come for Christmas Day if he liked. Or for Boxing Day. Or for New Year. Daddy, I told them, would rather spend all three dates flat on his back with a bottle of Bourbon. But, as they insisted, I would bring down my lover and her child.

'What do you mean,' said Susan rather crossly, '"lover"?'

'I mean "lover",' I said, 'you know – like "private detective" or "criminal" or "hero" or "villain".'

She sniffed down the phone at me.

'I forgot', I said, 'that you liked life to conform to your principles of good taste.'

Ella didn't want to come.

'Can't we jus' carry on like this?' she said.

'Our relationship must mature and grow,' I said. 'You must meet my ex-wife and her boyfriend.'

She laughed and said she'd come.

Saul and Susan had moved to a place just outside Uckfield in Sussex. It was the week before Christmas, and by now every single shop and stall was wishing you good cheer. It wasn't snowing. There was a cold rain, turning to sleet coming down over the neat Sussex landscape as I turned off the Eastbourne road towards the place Saul had bought. LITTLE HAMLYN the letter had said. I supposed that meant it was a spread of at least twelve acres.

The countryside had a bad effect on Ella. She smoked in a spectacularly self-destructive manner as I pushed the Cortina round folksy side roads and across patches of tamed moorland. Then, as we passed a sign that read LITTLE HAMLYN 2 MILES (the last one had told us it was one and three quarters), she sat bolt upright and told me to stop the car.

'I can't take this,' she said. 'Stop the car.'

'What's up?'

'She doesn't want to see your new scrubber. Her and the nice little kiddies. Forget it. Let's go back.'

She was quite extraordinarily vehement and positive in her demands.

'Look Ella – '

'Go back.'

'What's the matter?'

'Everything's the matter.'

I stopped the car. In the back I saw Tommy watching us cannily. He hardly ever spoke but I was constantly aware of his gaze, shifting between the two of us. Ella lit another cigarette. We had stopped opposite a red-brick oast house, outside which were parked three sports cars and an estate car. Just in case there was any doubt about it, the owner of the place had had a sign put up that said THE OAST HOUSE outside the front door. The sleet had turned back to rain.

'Tell me,' I said, 'you and Dave Abbott – '

'Shut up about it cancher?' she said. 'Shut up about me and Dave and Stan. You wouldn't understand it, O.K.?'

'Fine,' I said.

There was a long silence. Then she said,

'O.K.'

Saul had bought a house that uniquely expressed his personality. It was large, in an aimless, rather desperate sort of way. It had the air of a too hastily adopted child. There were too many turrets, too many gables, too many garages and far too much garden for anyone to *use* – they were there, presumably, to feature in some brochure Saul was writing about the place. 'Three-hundred acre gardens, twelve bathrooms, eight kitchens. Would suit estate agent with delusions of grandeur . . . . '

He had started to get to my children. They were wearing pastel track suits, and all of them, with the exception of Rupert, looked as if they were on their way to an expensive public school. Which, I later discovered, they were.

'We've got them down for Ampthill,' said Saul. 'Is that O.K.?'

'Is that a race meeting?' I said.

Saul laughed. He had a great sense of humour.

Susan and Saul gave us warm dry sherry in one of the many rooms on the ground floor (the principal function of the rooms seemed to be to house the appalling furniture Saul had bought). After a decent interval, I said I might take the children out to lunch.

'Don't want to,' said Ben.

Ben's accent seemed to have got more up-market since I had last seen him.

I put my arms round him anyway.

'Go on Benny,' said Saul, 'you'll love it. Really you will.'

I got up and stood looking out at the garden. There seemed to be no limit to the garden. Just as the rooms seemed designed to hold furniture, so the garden seemed designed to employ gardeners. I couldn't see them but I knew they were out there somewhere, looking gnarled and canny.

'Take them to Julie's place,' said Saul, 'lovely roadhouse. Super for kids.'

Ella was looking as if she was about to be sick. I began to shepherd the kids towards the door. They didn't want to go. They didn't want to see Daddy even though it was nearly Christmas. They – you could tell – wanted to get straight on into the space suit, the Go-Kart and the pool table that Saul had doubtless purchased for them. He knew what kids like. Cash preferably. Or, in severe cases, high quality consumer goods.

I gazed down at my children as we went out to the car. Ella hadn't spoken since I had introduced her, when we first came in.

'So nice to see you, Mrs. Peace,' said Saul; 'so nice to

meet a friend of Charles.'

That was too much.

'Stop fucking patronising her, can't you?' I snapped.

He looked genuinely hurt.

'I'm sorry, Charles,' he said, 'I . . . . '

Miserably I loaded the children into the car. Maybe I had misjudged the guy. Maybe I was as much of a snob as he was. Christ, he was probably from the same social class as her come to think of it.

The kids didn't talk much in the car, but, after a while, Ben decided it was safe to smile. He told me he was going to a new school. I asked him what it was like. He told me there were a lot of foreign boys there. Some of the foreign boys, he told me, were quite nice really. Tommy said there was a boy at his school who couldn't speak English. Then they were away into a lively session of pre-secondary school racism. Ella still wasn't speaking. Because I couldn't think what else to do, I stopped a passing yokel and asked him the way to Julie's place.

'Oh yah,' said the yokel, 'Julie's place. Frahfly good. Taramasalada.'

This he seemed to find extremely funny. Eventually I got the directions out of him, and when I had run them through an internal descrambling device, deduced it was two or three miles down the road.

'Dave Abbot – ' I began, but Ella cut me off.

'What's the matter?' she said. 'Do you think I killed him or something?'

'I think', I said, 'that Abbott may have been mixed up with a certain Mr. Ainsworth in some dirty deal. He's been feeding me information. I think perhaps to protect himself.'

'I don't know about any of that,' said Ella, 'I told you. I won't talk about Stan.'

'Did you love him?'

She laughed. Discussing this side of her relationship,

clearly, was far too interesting to be classed as 'talking about him.'

'I stayed with him,' she said enigmatically.

Julie's place was the sort of establishment people like Saul frequent when they want to get out for a night. Perhaps because its décor might have been conceived and executed by them. There were a lot of plants and a lot of screens and a lot of waitresses, peeping shyly out of the foliage, waving menus the size of prayer mats. The clientèle were making a great impression on each other, and on the management. I got a table by the lavatory, for which I was humbly grateful.

'What's it to be kids?'

'Ketchup,' said Toby.

'Anything on the ketchup?'

They liked this. Things were getting better.

'Chips,' said Ben.

Ella had got hold of Rupert and was propping him up in a chair. He gazed at her, pop-eyed. She seemed genuinely amused by him. I remembered Susan's agonised face at the window as we drove away and wondered why it should be so difficult to love the mother of one's children. When her only fault, essentially, had been to love them. I'd turned her into Hausfrau Susan hadn't I? I'd created the image, been unfaithful to it, and then acted hurt when it had risen up in its own right, and devoured me.

What's the matter with you, Charlie? Don't you want to? Don't you . . . ?

I looked across at Ella. She wasn't looking at the children. She was looking across to the window. At the table there were three men in dark suits. They looked at first like businessmen having one of those meaningless lunchtime conversations. They had the sort of solemnity that is needed to justify the expense of thirty or forty pounds of someone else's money. They looked as if they were eating fried pound notes.

'That's one of them,' Ella said.

'One of who?'

'Stan's mates. The foreign . . . . '

She didn't finish the sentence. One of them was getting to his feet and going out of the door. Any doubts she had had about talking about her late husband did not extend to these gentlemen. It was quite clear that their presence here scared her. I wasn't going to learn anything from cross questioning her on the subject. I got up from the table.

'Where are you going?' said Ben.

I noticed an expression of unmixed admiration in his eyes. So help me, I said,

'I'm after some bad men.'

'Robbers?'

'That's it. Robbers.'

'Great,' he said. 'Robbers'.

I've always found that children understand my profession better than adults. They have, in my experience, a clearer sense of moral priorities. Feeling as if I was doing the right thing I went out of the door and into the narrow lane below the restaurant.

I saw the man Ella had pointed out, walking briskly off to the right, his hands in the pockets of his overcoat. He looked, I had to admit, like a man about to pick up a message from a hollow tree. As I watched he rounded the corner and disappeared. I ran down on to the road and followed him.

When I came round the first bend he was nowhere to be seen. There was a stile about ten yards down on the left and just the other side of it, a large black saloon car. I went up to the stile and looked over into the field. There was no-one there. As far as I could see there was no-one in the car either. I climbed over the stile and moved into the field. Over to the right was a small clump of trees. For a moment I thought I heard a crack. I stopped. Had it come from the trees or from the road? When I got to the edge of the wood I saw that there was no-one there. It was no more than twenty yards deep. On the other side was a ploughed field, naked, deserted.

I turned back to the road. Slowly, cautiously, I climbed the stile. I didn't want to go towards the car but I supposed I better had.

It turned out to be unlocked. On the front seat was a pile of books, mainly paperbacks. On the covers, the writing appeared to be Cyrillic. I could make out none of the words. I got out and went round to the boot. That to my surprise, was open as well. I pushed it back and found I was looking down at three black suitcases. I reached for the handle of one of them and moved the case slightly. Whatever was in it was extremely heavy. I leaned further in to the boot to get both hands under it, and something hard hit me on the back of the head.

I turned and tried to do the Charlie Alexander Wound Your Opponent For Life With The Index Finger Of Your Left Hand Technique. I was shaping up nicely to the opening stages of this routine when I found my knees were buckling and I was unable to see anything but a red mist. Then I fell forward on to the road.

I didn't die or go to heaven. I woke up, half an hour later, in the bar of Julie's place.

'What happened?' waitresses kept asking.

'I fell,' I said.

Ella seemed embarrassed more than anything else. After we had taken the children back and were driving homeward through the December evening, to my surprise she talked to me about her dead husband.

'He could be so sweet,' she said, looking out at the dark fields, 'so sweet.'

Then she started to move her hand in concentric circles along the top of my thigh. In the back, Tommy was asleep.

'Am I sweet?' I said.

'Yes,' she said, 'you're sweet.'

This thought depressed me.

The next morning I got a call from Dave Abbott. He said he had found an address for me. One of Peace's companions on the Ruskin course. Peter Stevens, a miner. He was working, Abbott said, at Betteshanger colliery in Kent. He'd spoken to him for me and Stevens hadn't remembered anything that would be useful.

'Oh,' I said.

'Who's on the phone?' said Ella.

'It's your friend Mr. Abbott,' said I.

'He's not my friend,' she said.

'What was the address again?' I said.

'Do you need it?' said Abbott.

'I'm not sure,' I said.

I didn't press him. If I needed to find Mr. Stevens myself I could do so. What interested me more was that tone I had caught in Abbott's voice. It was the one I remembered from the seafront that day in Eastbourne. He sounded to me as if he was frightened.

'Ella,' I said, 'were you having an affair with Dave

Abbott?'

She laughed.

'What gives you that idea?'

'The way you look when I mention him. Or when he calls.'

'No,' she said. Then she added, 'You nosey bastard.'

The next week was dull. Nobody tried to kill me. Nobody threw a brick through my window or left threatening messages on my answering machine. My Japanese friend rang and said that he had decided to stay in this country. Would I accept a thousand pounds for my trouble? I said I would. Ella and Tommy and I did all the things that I had once done with Susan. We walked on Barnes Common and fed the ducks and drank in the White Hart, while Maggie looked after the boy. She had discovered that she and he had a common interest: violent television programmes. Things weren't better or worse than they had been with Susan. They were just different. What I was frightened of was the day when they started to get the same.

'Leave it alone cancher?' she said to me one night.

'What?'

'All of it. Stan. The Union. All of it.'

'He liked all that didn't he?'

'It was his life the bloody union was.'

That night on the television they said that the D.W.U. were suing each other. Mr. Prothero, said a man who looked as if he did not like having to talk about this sort of thing, was suing Mr. Harris.

'You see?' said Ella.

'See what?'

'They're all as bad as each other.'

Next day I went hospital visiting.

Paul Tucker made a flamboyant invalid. He had his leg up in plaster, a pile of cards above his bed and every single daily newspaper spread out before him. He was holding a transistor radio to his left ear. Beside his bed, in a white mac, was Mr. Smith. He nodded when he saw me.

'D.W.U. IN COURTROOM BATTLE HORROR,' he said. 'COMMUNIST CHIEF RIGGED VOTES SAYS MODERATE CHIEF.'

'Did he?' I said.

Tucker removed the radio from his ear.

'No more than anyone else,' he said.

He turned to Smith. 'Are you doing it?'

'Think so,' said Smith.

Tucker winced.

'Could you fetch the good sister for me, Mr. Smith?' he said.

Smith inclined his head.

'If you two want to talk . . . ,' he said.

'Thanks.'

As soon as he had gone, Tucker said,

'Why didn't you call earlier?'

'I was checking some things out.'

'Such as . . . .'

I told him about the Ruskin course. Then I told him about Dave Abbott.

'I can't tie up this Pension Fund deal,' I said. 'I think it's more complicated than that. I think Abbott may be involved.'

Tucker leaned close to me.

'Listen,' he said, 'I have a source within the Union. Very well placed. Who maintains he can show me documents which incriminate not only Harry Ainsworth in a whole range of semi-legal transactions in relation to finance inside and outside the D.W.U. but also Owen Harris the left General Secretary of the Union and a whole load of other left-wingers on the national executive.'

There was something in Tucker's expression that told me

he was doubtful about this story.

'But you don't believe your source right?'

'I'm checking it out.'

'If it incriminates prominent left-wingers, it must be unrealistic and untrue, right?'

Tucker sniffed. I gave him my right-wing speech about how the Trades Union movement had once stood for integrity and decency but had been betrayed into greed and complacency by post-war affluence. I gave him the benefit of my two days' research into the D.W.U. (which I knew would irritate him still further). I even quoted one of his own remarks back to him, along the lines of the D.W.U. being a symbol of the current crisis in the Labour movement. This was too much for Tucker, and, as I had hoped, he went further than he intended.

'Listen young man there is a *war* on the Distributive Workers' Union. Harris is being sued by a gentleman named Prothero, a creature whose political views have the sophistication of those of a Dobermann Pinscher.'

'I.e. a right winger.'

'You are beginning to show the glimmerings of political understanding, my friend.'

I saw Smith loping back along the ward. He was carrying a bottle of Lucozade.

'You think', I said quickly, 'your source may be part of a smear campaign associated with this move against Harris. Your source being . . . . '

'A little to the right of left of centre.'

I went on thinking out loud. Smith had opened the Lucozade bottle and was sniffing it glumly.

'And if your theory is correct, the Pension Fund story could be part of the same campaign. I got that from Abbott. Let's say Abbott was your source. He's putting pressure on Ainsworth and the left, Stan Peace cops his mischief-making activities and gets done in for his pains. By Abbott.

Who is also an old friend ha ha ha of Ella Peace.'

'It's more serious than that Charlie,' said Tucker. 'If it were that simple I'd be going for Abbott. Not that I agree that he is my source. The fact is that Harry Ainsworth is in deep trouble.'

I couldn't afford to think about our friend Ainsworth. Suspecting two people at the same time in any enquiry is a little like trying to juggle and ride a bike at the same time. I accepted a glass of Lucozade from Smith. To my surprise it tasted like Lucozade.

'There *is* gin in it,' said Smith, 'but Lucozade is pretty powerful stuff.'

I needed to know about this mysterious right-wing gentleman, Mr. Prothero. If Prothero was up to some skulduggery, I ought to get a look at him. Was being ousted from one's post as General Secretary of a not very important union worth killing for, though? Well, not in my case. I would probably have killed anyone in order to get out of it; from my observation of the D.W.U. comrades it had become clear to me that there was nothing in life, as far as they were concerned, to compare with sitting up on a platform arguing about Rule 45z. The shadowy, elusive nature of my murder victim came from the fact that his life had been swallowed up in politics. In order to understand him I was going to have to understand the thing I'd avoided for twenty or so years.

Once, a long time ago, I was a member of the Communist Party. It was a bit like being in care.

It turned out that Smith was on his way to the High Court to observe the very case in action. I asked if I could come with him. He told me I was welcome. Tucker watched us go with the expression of a St. Bernard dog forced into early retirement in the middle of a particularly interesting blizzard.

The High Court turned out to be a rather homey little place. I had imagined vast distances between the protagonists, but instead it was rather closer to some American court scene. The officials of the court, however, were in fancy dress, and the judge was the usual example of a dirty old man in a wig. Up on the stand an unfortunate man in a shabby suit was being given a hard time by a keen young barrister. Eton and Oxford meets unemployed packer. And Eton and Oxford was in drag.

'In areas twenty-nine and thirty,' the barrister was saying in a menacing voice, 'the votes were counted by . . . .'

'Which is Prothero?' I whispered.

Smith indicated a tall, pinched-looking man. I remembered his face now. But he did not interest me as much as the man sitting next to him in urgent consultation. It was Dave Abbott. Up on the stand the unemployed packer was being given a harder and harder time. They replaced him with Owen Harris. Mr. Harris did not look as happy as he had in the Leisure Halls, Eastbourne. The debate seemed to be about who exactly had counted the votes in an obscure district of Newcastle.

'What's the electoral procedure of the D.W.U.?' I whispered to Smith.

'Complex,' he said.

I wasn't really interested in who was in the right. What interested me was that Abbott should have been at such pains to conceal his political affiliations. His presence with Prothero helped to explain his helpful but evasive attitude to me, not to mention his hostility to Ainsworth. And there was Ella . . . .

I looked at Abbott's profile. Any middle-range executive of any corporation. After promotion. Presumably appointments in the D.W.U. – like appointments in any organisation – depended on patronage. His convex blue eyes were shining with the close range sincerity of a disc-jockey.

Smith was scribbling in a notebook. Up on the stand Mr. Harris was talking about the democracy of working-class organisations. The barrister smirked at this. Perhaps he thought Mr. Harris was referring to football teams or Christmas clubs. For sure he wasn't talking about the High Court. As I watched Abbott and Prothero, I felt a prickle of anger as unreliable as love. Abbott. Abbott. Why had Abbott not allowed me near the mysterious Peter Stevens, on that course at Ruskin all those years ago?

In the middle of a particularly smart series of remarks from Prothero's lawyer, Abbott got up to go. With a whispered adieu to Smith, I followed him. He went out of the court and turned up towards the Strand. He was in a hurry. Then, to my horror, from a side turning came the person he was clearly intending to meet. They didn't kiss but there was something intimate and conspiratorial about the way they greeted each other. It was Ella.

I watched them talk from the safety of a shop doorway. They seemed to be arguing. After a while Abbott tried to take her arm. She brushed it away. Then she turned and ran off into the crowd. I didn't follow her. I waited until Abbott had turned back towards the Court and walked towards him.

He was as easy with me as he had been with my answering machine. Good old Dave Abbott. Slightly to the right of left-of-centre Dave Abbott. Mr. Nice-guy. The coming man.

'Hullo there Charles.'

I smiled. I thought I'd spoil his day for him.

'I've got a very interesting lead', I said, 'on those names I gave you.'

He didn't even blink.

'Great,' he said, 'great.'

Then I walked up towards Soho with a cheery wave. Almost as easy as good old Dave. I wanted to see Mo Allen. Urgently.

Mo was still sitting at her viewing machine. It was small black children she was looking at now, with bellies the size of an executive paunch and ribs that looked as if the meat had been carved off them. She had the same expression I remembered from my last visit. Wistful. As if she wanted to be part of the image on the screen and not here in a drab room over a vegetable market. She seemed pleased to see me.

'You're one of the most politically unreliable people I've ever had in here,' she said.

'Will you do me a favour?' I said.

She'd already gone to the shelf and got down that square green box. She didn't put it on the machine this time. Instead she motioned me through to a small box-like room with a screen about four foot across.

'This is the dubbing theatre,' she said, giving a gloomy laugh. As soon as the images came back I knew we were going to get somewhere this time. Grainy, oversized, those distant faces were palpable at last. I even had a picture of Mo herself behind the camera as it swayed from pub to river to dreary lecture room. And then we came to the section I wanted. The man with the glass up at his mouth. The man I was sure I had recognised. I asked her to stop the film.

'That man,' I said, 'the one you said was interested in Ella.'

'There was this feller from the town who – '

'This one,' I said, 'this one.'

'Can't recall his name. He was a – '

She stopped. She came up to my side and the two of us stood, noses to the image on the screen. I felt like peeling it off and shaking it back to life. Mo wrinkled her forehead in concentration.

'*I* know . . . . '

'What?'

'Abbott. Dave Abbott. That was it. Because it was always

“call me Dave”. You know? Dave bloody Abbott.’

‘Ms. Allen,’ I said, ‘you’re beautiful. Did anyone ever tell you that?’

And I kissed her on both cheeks.

The D.W.U. case was written up in the papers every day. I couldn't relate the forbidding paragraphs to the drama of that tiny room or the names at the head of the stories to the correspondents I had come to know. Christmas had been and gone. I had a letter from Ben that looked as if it had been written by a mental patient. In it he told me that Saul had bought him an At At snow walker, a bicycle, three guns and a snooker table. There was a letter from Toby too but he didn't go in for details of Saul's recent purchases. He drew me a picture of the sun and the sky. I sellotaped it on to the kitchen wall, and when Maggie came round to play poker that night she burst into tears.

Ella went out a lot, which suited Maggie. She didn't like Ella. I could start to feel the beginning of the old problem. A feeling of nervousness every time she touched me, a desire to take evasive action when she came through the bedroom door in touching, artless sets of matching underwear. I didn't ask her where she went most nights, although I was frightened that I knew without having to ask.

Paul Tucker was out of hospital. He reported the news of the industrial scene from a wheelchair. He still refused to confirm that Abbott was his source for the story that incriminated Ainsworth and his friends. I began to wonder whether there was more to Mr. Abbott's routine than Pension Funds, but I no longer shared my theories with Tucker. January inched forward, week by week, grim as a funeral.

Susan wrote to me too. She said she hoped I was happy. She wanted me to know that she was happy. She was really deliriously happy. She felt that the world was beginning anew. She actually used the word 'anew'. I reflected that Saul must be having a bad effect on her prose style. What I couldn't take was the feeling that it was all about to start to happen again, that Ella and I were about to start the same round of rows and reconciliations, the same arguments that were not supposed to be about 'it' but *were* about 'it'.

Well, you know all about 'it', don't you? Sex. It. I'm terrific at sex. For the first three weeks or so I'm great at it. I do all the things Cosmopolitan tells you to do. I moan and I groan and I am tender and I indulge in lots and lots of foreplay and afterplay and I make sure everybody has a nice time and serve myself last like you were always told to at the home they put me in when my mother died, and then, after a while, I lose interest. I don't want to moan and groan any more. Every time the woman comes through the door in her black underwear (which I'm bored with now because I've seen it before) I don't think, 'Oh here's another chance to renew our relationship's physical meaning'. I think, 'I'd rather have a nice cup of tea'.

Some women I've been involved with have asked me questions about what they call, with scrupulous delicacy, my 'inability to perform'. Or, in other words my 'impotence'. I tell them I'm not unable to perform. It's just that I am unable to perform with them. They understandably resent this and often use quite harsh words to describe my lack of enthusiasm. I sit and stare at the wall and wait until they go away. Then there's another woman.

Some last longer. Susan lasted nearly eight years. But then, I never loved her. Not in the way I was beginning to love Ella. It was always much much worse when I fell in love with them.

In the middle of a particularly bad week at the end of the month I went to see Dave Abbott. I felt like a little confrontation. He was now something called the Metropolitan Regional Assistant Organiser. They had given him an office in a new block at an address in the Harrow Road. He said he would be really pleased to see me. He really wanted to have a little chat. He'd really tried to get hold of those names I'd given him and was amazed I'd had such luck.

How were they of help? I tried to give the impression that they hadn't named him as being on that course with Peace at Ruskin all those years ago. I wanted it to be a nice surprise for him.

In the paper on the way down I read that the election of Mr. Owen Harris had been declared null and void. The person writing the story – who wasn't known to me – opined that the 'moderate' candidates would now sweep the board as almost every post on the Executive Committee would now be up for re-selection. Mr. Prothero described it as a victory for democracy. Mr. Harris said it was a blow against democracy. I wondered whether Abbott counted as a moderate.

His new office was a perfect contrast to the one where I had first met Ainsworth. It was all glass and louvre doors and Venetian blinds. There were no posters advertising trips to Bulgaria. In fact the graphic design of the posters on the wall was so tasteful it was impossible to tell what, if anything, they were about. Abbott was smoking a cigar and had his feet on the desk.

'Well,' I said, 'what happens to you now?'

'How do you mean, old son?' he said.

I told him how I meant. He grinned.

'I'll do O.K.,' he said.

Then he read me a short lecture on contemporary politics. Things were changing (I gulped at this insight). We in the D.W.U. must change with them. Take the Newlands car company. The centre of their membership, the heart of the union. The left had involved them in a damaging strike up there. Nearly bankrupt the union. They couldn't afford strikes. They had to protect their members by more subtle and complex ways. They had to go to the negotiating table. The old divisions between right and left were breaking down. The –

I let this go on for as long as I could stand it. Then I said, 'And what'll you do? Take yourself out to lunch?'

He sat up, surprised by my tone.

'Why,' I said, 'didn't you tell me you knew Stan Peace all those years ago at Ruskin? I think he was killed because of something that happened then. Something to do with a woman. Why didn't you want to let me meet any of the names I got from Mo Allen? Because they might remember something about you? Why were you feeding me crap about the Pension Fund? Why? Because all you were interested in was getting a better job with Prothero's mob.'

'Charles,' said Abbott, 'I have seen papers which –'

'Papers nothing,' I said. 'You're just an opportunist little shit and – "

He seemed to have lost his tan. I was coming towards him round the desk, my hands clenching and unclenching. I saw myself in the window behind him, broken boxer's nose and my eyes large and baleful. Though I say it myself, I looked quite frightening.

'You think I killed him don't you?' said Abbott backing away towards one of the potted plants. 'Well, you don't know the half of it do you? Row about a woman? SAY IT. IT'S ELLA PEACE, RIGHT? YOU DON'T KNOW THE HALF OF IT. ASK ELLA PEACE WHO'S BEEN GIVING HER ONE ALL THESE YEARS. GO ON ASK HER. SOMEONE'S GOT HER SEWN UP AND IT ISN'T YOU, IS IT? GO ON ASK HER . . . .'

I got hold of his jacket and threw him across the room. He landed in a heap by one of the futuristic waste-paper baskets the D.W.U. had seen fit to provide him. I went over to him, picked him up and hit him hard in the face.

'It's you, isn't it, you adaptable little bastard?' I said.

His mouth was bleeding. He fell to the floor again and I pulled him up by those oh so impeccable lapels. He looked sullen and tired.

'Go on then,' he said, 'go on. You don't know the fucking

half of it. Ask your precious bloody Ella.'

I felt sick with myself. Big butch Charlie Alexander. Nobody messes him about. Even six-year-old boys aren't safe. I had a mental image of me shaking Ben one night and of Susan screaming and screaming at me to stop. I let Mr. Abbott go. He did not fall to the floor but lay against the wall wiping his mouth. I remembered he and Ella in that street outside the Law Courts. Oh come on. Not her. Please not her. *You're going to have to go over for it sweetheart.* If you live your life by the conventions of pulp fiction, don't expect to complain of the endings it dishes out to you. We get the clichés we deserve. I turned round and went out to the lifts without saying another word. As I was waiting, Abbott came out. He looked suddenly older.

'Listen,' he said, 'I need to talk to you. I must. I don't think I'm safe. I want to talk to you.'

'Put it in a letter,' I said. And went down to the January night.

Like I said – when I'm involved it affects my judgement. I could have saved myself a lot of trouble by waiting, even for thirty seconds. But I didn't.

Ella was in when I got back to the flat. She was sitting in the front room smoking and reading a magazine called *Home Buyers*. I didn't waste any time.

'Are you having an affair with Dave Abbott?' I said.

That seemed to amuse her.

'Are you?'

'No.'

'Look why didn't you tell me you'd known him all those years ago, when you met Stan?'

'I don't talk to you about any of that. You know the rules.'

'But why not?'

'You think I killed him, doncher?'

'I don't want to think that.'

She got up and put out her cigarette.

'If you want to know. The night he was killed I was out. And you know who I was out with? Dave Abbott.'

'You were having an affair with him.'

'I DIDN'T SAY THAT!'

I looked around the flat. It was funny. Neither she nor Tommy had made any impact on it. Whereas Susan would have started to put up pictures, curtains, shelves, this woman was like me. Rootless, hopeless. And that was the way I wanted her, the way you want certain moods or scenes when you're adolescent. When she left – and I was starting to realise that she was going to go – she would leave nothing. I sighed and turned back to her.

'Abbott implied there was someone else. Always had been.'

'Did he now?'

She was crying. I couldn't bear that. I went over to her and put my arm round her. I patted her shoulder but I couldn't do it right. It felt like I was testing a bed in a department store. She looked up at me, her ragged, over-blonded hair across her eyes, tears all the way down her thin cheeks.

'I do love you, Charlie. I don't know what that means but I do love you. I want to be with you all the time. It's funny. I loved Stan in my way too but . . . . '

'I'm sorry,' I said.

I tried to smile.

'I'll find out. I will. Even if it turns out it was the bleeding C.I.A., I'll – '

There was a knock, then a ring at the door. I froze. The thing had been done, it seemed to me, with sudden and unnecessary violence. Then the bell started one long ring. A one-note drone that would not stop. I went to the window. Down the street a van was drawing out. I went to the landing.

'Charlie be careful – '

'What of – '

'He – '

'Abbott?'

She was looking at me, her mouth open. She looked that way Abbott had looked on the seafront at Eastbourne. Sheer, stark terror. Who was at the damn door? I started down the stairs. I could see a shape through the frosted glass of the pane. I didn't stop. Ella was at the top of the stairs.

'Charlie – '

And that damn bell! It wouldn't stop. On and on and on. I paced the length of the hall and yanked back the door.

They had trussed Abbott up like a chicken. He fell forwards into the hall like some item of discarded luggage and landed at my feet. His eyes were wide open in a wild stare but I didn't pay any attention to the eyes. It wasn't even the blood on his face and shirtfront or the hands, splayed at a weird angle. It wasn't even the fact that the side of his head had been hammered at by someone. It was the sheer frenzy with which it had been done that recalled the body I had found in that flat on the Wearing Estate. The way the skin and bone had been attacked again and again and again. Cratered like a candle. The work of a madman.

PART THREE

It was time to talk to Mr. Ainsworth. That meant contacting Paul Tucker. It wasn't difficult to find him. The quality newspapers were carrying stories about the new regime at the D.W.U. As far as I could see Mr. Ainsworth had not lost his job. It was simply that his masters had changed. In Mr. Smith's paper I read a headline that said IT'S ALL OUT BROTHER IN NEWLANDS UNION ROW. Underneath this headline was a story written by Mr. Smith. To my surprise he actually wrote as he talked, but here his resemblance to D. H. Lawrence ended. The story began:

> The trouble-torn Newlands car factory took a turn for the better today with a new statement from new moderate D.W.U. union boss Ray Prothero. 'We are not in a position of confrontation on the issues of manning and wage levels,' Mr. Prothero said at his Croydon Headquarters. 'Confrontation is what has got us into this mess.'
>
> COMMUNIST ISOLATED
>
> Mr. Harry Ainsworth, the man at the storm centre of the strife-hit plant retains his job as district organiser responsible for the factory. But how long will he and his fellow stewards hold the loyalty of their members at Newlands, now that the Executive has swung in favour of the moderate course? Ainsworth, 52, is a prominent member of the Communist Party and has made no secret of the fact that there is little love lost between him and moderate Prothero.

I wondered whether Smith had been drinking too much Lucozade. A phone call to Tucker established that he and prose stylist Smith, 38, would be outside the front gates of the Headquarters of the D.W.U. in Croydon at 10.30 on

February 3rd.

'You spend your life hanging around the outside of buildings, Paul,' I said.

'I thought private detectives did that,' said Paul, 'taking pictures of other people's wives.'

'I'm not that sort of private detective,' I said. 'I only handle issues of national importance.'

The D.W.U. Headquarters proved to be a Tudor building in a large garden in a quiet street near East Croydon station. It reminded me of an old folks home. There were two or three journalists hanging around the front drive among whom I recognised Tucker, Smith and a familiar face above a car-coat that turned out to be Ted Chabot.

'I've heard,' said Chabot, 'that Prothero is wanted for sex offences with young children.'

'How young?' said Tucker.

'Six?' said Chabot in a wheedling, hopeful tone.

'No story,' said Tucker. 'Tells us nothing new about Prothero.'

At this moment a group of men in suits marched up the drive. I noticed Prothero among them. Most of the journalists started after them down the drive. Tucker and Smith stayed where they were. Then from the other side of the house I saw another group emerge among whom I saw Ainsworth and Owen Harris.

'What's this?' I said, 'the changing of the guard?'

'Sort of,' said Tucker.

He went up to the group. I saw Ainsworth look in my direction.

'Gentlemen,' said Tucker, 'will you allow my newspaper to buy you a substantial lunch?'

Ainsworth gestured at me.

'Not him,' he said.

'He's O.K., Harry,' said Tucker. 'He wants to talk to you about Abbott.'

Ainsworth flinched slightly. I remembered dragging Abbott's body out into the back of the car, and driving it to the river that night, with Ella beside me. We had left it on a patch of waste ground out West, beyond Hampton Court. I looked every day in the papers, but saw no mention of Abbott's name or of the death. It could take the rest of our natural lives for the police to tie Abbott to me or Ella. I've great respect for the police, mind you. I think they're marvellous with animals and young children, but for anything requiring sustained intellectual effort I prefer to rely on myself.

'Who did he know?' I said to Ella that night. 'Friends, relatives . . . .'

'He didn't have no friends,' Ella had said, as we drove back towards town, 'except me. No family either.'

'Were you having an affair with him?'

'No, Charlie. It was just someone to talk to. I was alone most of the time. Stan was out at meetings. I dunno . . . Abbott called round. He'd always fancied me. Since . . . .'

'Since when?'

'I don't want to talk about it.'

'Fine.'

And there had been no letters from little old ladies in Leeds wondering what had happened to darling Dave. No mention from anyone. Fresh, dry-cleaned Dave Abbott had just disappeared the way people do. All that was left of him were some bloodstains on my hall carpet, and the sudden uneasiness in the eyes of the likes of Harry Ainsworth.

Tucker took them to an Indian restaurant near the station. I was placed next to Ainsworth. While Tucker and Smith talked with the others I carried on an almost whispered conversation with Ainsworth.

'What happened to Abbott?'

'Somebody killed him.'

Ainsworth breathed in. I couldn't understand his expression for a moment. Then I saw it was one of relief.

'Look young man,' he said, 'when you came to my office that day. I thought you were with him. If you want to know, Mr. Abbott was . . . .'

'Was what?'

'He was blackmailing me.'

This news did not surprise me as much as it was supposed to. Neither did I think for one moment that the quaint, nearly elderly man beside me had done what had been done to Abbott.

'What was the reason he – '

'That's all I'm saying. You're on the wrong trail. That was a personal matter, O.K.? If you are, as Paul says, after whoever it was who killed Stan Peace you may ask me about anything you choose. But I won't discuss . . . .'

I wondered what it was the poor old bastard had done. I tried to picture Mr. Ainsworth on Wimbledon Common in a fetching leather jerkin. Then I saw one of Smith's headlines. COMMUNIST IN INDECENCY CHARGE HORROR. What must life be like, I wondered for a Communist in the news? Not a lot of fun. Not exactly the feeling that the nation's press were giving you a fair hearing. There seemed a total discrepancy between the group of us in the restaurant and the headlines that shouted about the disruptive, the inhuman, the alien creatures of political demonology. I began to understand why it was a man like Ainsworth should feel the need to scream occasionally. Presumably the intention of those who ran the *Sun*, the *Daily Mail* and the rest was that he should have some form of nervous breakdown. Judging from his nervous little repertoire of mannerisms, his argumentativeness, his rapid switches from bonhomie to anger, he was in the middle of one at the moment. I didn't press him on the subject of his real, or notional, or at any rate blackmailable crime. I listened to the chatter of Tucker and the others.

'Next time,' said Harris, 'we really will sew up the constitution of the bloody Union.'

Ainsworth put down his knife and fork and gazed gloomily across the restaurant. In the far corner was a middle-aged man and a woman who looked like his secretary. He was trying to kiss her. There was a smear of yellow gravy down his chin. Outside, the pedestrians of Croydon staggered home in the February afternoon.

'I think his bloody wife killed him,' said Ainsworth.

I didn't attempt to answer this. I knew he was talking about Stan Peace. Instead I said, not for professional reasons but because I wanted to make the dead man real again, to start to understand the shadow I was chasing, 'What was he like? Stan Peace.'

To my horror Ainsworth's eyes filled with tears.

'I loved him,' he said. 'I bloody loved him.'

This time I followed Ainsworth properly. If I could have said with certainty that Abbott was working on his own, I thought I could have eliminated the two of them (I had no doubt that the same man had killed both Abbott and Peace). But there remained the suspicion that he had been acting under orders. After all there were plenty of other people who had an interest in removing Mr.Ainsworth and his friends. Mr. Prothero for a start.

Ella seemed to want to come with me. In fact, she didn't seem to want to leave me alone at all. If I went to the shops she asked to come with me. She never left the house except with me and her visits away had ceased, which made me certain that it had been Abbott that she was seeing. On one of the rare occasions when she went out by herself, I said,

'What's happened to me all of a sudden?'

'I'm your insurance policy,' she said.

Maggie didn't come and play poker any more. She looked after Tommy but rarely talked to me. I saw her once through her window in what looked like a Yoga position, her mauve skirt up by her waist, her made-up face strained with effort. Why, I thought, do I surround myself with sad people? Because I'm one of them of course.

I asked Ella why she wanted to come with me when I went after Ainsworth but she just laughed. Then she said,

'I don't want you to wind up like our friend Abbott.'

I wondered whether she was on the verge of a nervous breakdown as well. I wouldn't have blamed her. I sometimes felt like sobbing when conductors asked me for the fare.

I spent nearly a week watching the D.W.U. district office where Ainsworth worked. Nothing much happened. He came and went. I got to know where he went for lunch, which turned out to be, on several occasions, his car. I saw him go to the local pub with three men who looked exactly like him. I sat in the Cortina and talked to Ella about everything apart from Stan Peace and Dave Abbott. I talked to her about her mother and father and about how it was having a baby, and I talked rather too much about what it was like for me and women. How I grabbed at them as they passed. How I couldn't make anything last. I told her about my life too. About the club I used to run and the play I was going to write and about a whole load of other things that were probably lies meant to impress her and make her stay. I lie about everything. I call myself any number of things. You mustn't believe everything I say.

At the end of the first week I struck lucky. Ainsworth came out of the office at twelve o'clock. He never did that. He was carrying a large black briefcase. For some reason I remembered that briefcase. He almost ran to his car, and I followed him as he pulled out into the main road.

He drove out towards Streatham.

'What's his game?' said Ella.

'I think he's going to meet someone I might want to meet.'

When he got to Streatham he parked the car near the ice rink and, still in that untypical hurry, he ran down a subway on the other side of the road. I ran after him. It wasn't until I had clattered down the stairs that I realised why he was running. He had seen me. Whoever it was he was meeting wasn't here. He thumped up the opposite steps and out on to Streatham High Street. I stayed close to him. Then he veered off the road and headed down another pedestrian subway. I vaulted down the stairs three at a time and caught him at the entrance to the tunnel. He turned to me and hurled the black briefcase at my stomach. It didn't hurt much. Except, when I opened it, there was about five hundred pounds in rolls of ones and fives.

'Where did this come from?' I said. 'The D.W.U. universal benevolent fund?'

Ainsworth was sweating. His face was the colour of arterial blood.

'Listen. I was just to leave the money. O.K.? Just to leave the money. Leave me alone can't you?'

'Who is it?' I said. 'You know it isn't Abbott, right? Because Abbott's dead.'

He breathed in and looked at me in a kind of triumph.

'Listen,' he said, 'if you want to know who's behind this don't waste your time following me from point to point. Ask the new and glorious leader of the Distributive Workers' Union what he's been doing. Ask Mr. Bloody Prothero. Ask him about the slice of Newlands he wants to get. Ask him about bloody Amtro.'

'Amtro?'

'Oh they're a property company I believe,' he said. 'They have beautiful brochures and pleasant offices. But no-one quite knows what they do.'

I picked up the briefcase and handed it back to him. I felt suddenly sorry for him.

'When I came into this movement,' he said, 'if you had a card you were out. I spent my youth in factories where to be a member of a Union was a punishable offence. I saw men sacked and bullied and tyrannised and treated like cattle. And now. Now we have people coming up through our movement who have the ethics of the Stock Exchange.'

'You shouldn't be a Trades Unionist, Mr. Ainsworth,' I said, 'you should be in the Pentecostal Church.'

'Ask Mr. Bloody Prothero,' he said, 'ask him about Amtro.'

Then he walked off through the subway. I wanted to tell him to take his briefcase and throw it at whoever was putting the bite on him but I did not do so. Whoever was taking money off Ainsworth, it seemed to me, was nothing to do with the Peace affair. It was some sad private business of his own, some unhappy private vice. How wrong I was. Everything in the Stan Peace affair hung together. Marx would have been proud of the way it all fitted. I let him go anyway and went back up to Ella who was playing the radio, in search of a station that gave her even louder, even more continuous music.

'Well?' she said.

'Did you ever go hunting?' I said.

'Can't say as I did,' she said.

'I went with my wife,' I said.

'I can believe it,' said Ella.

I started the car then.

'It's not a lot of fun,' I said.

I read the industrial news now as a matter of course. Places I had never even thought about became important to me. I worried about the merger at S.P.L. Engineering. I read the published words of Mr. Terry Duffy. I became a fan of the rapidly dwindling group of people in England engaged in making things other than video games. I remember one of Smith's stories that read:

> LASTING PEACE AT STATE OWNED PLANT?
>
> The troubled car manufacturers at Newlands today saw the chance of a new and permanent settlement when Mr. Ray Prothero . . . .

I began to wonder whether I had been too local in my view of the politics of the Peace affair. After all, what really mattered, as far as the big boys were concerned, was not the fate of one shop steward or of a few thousand workers but the profitability of the plant. Supposing there was a link between Prothero and . . . .

And who? Ainsworth had suggested a property company. I went to the library and tried to find traces of them. I could find none. Whoever Messrs. Amtro were they were extremely discreet. Then one evening, I came home to find a letter from Susan.

> Dear Charlie,
> The children are lonely without you! They miss their father. Where are you? Are you still a vagabond? I am very peaceful here. Although it is winter I feel as close as I ever did to country things. Saul is away on business and I look out at our garden and think. Please please come to see us all . . . .

Often stupid people write quite intelligently and vice versa. Still, I was somewhat disturbed by the vaguely Norse tone of this letter. I rang her that night. To my surprise, Saul answered.

'Hullo,' I said, 'I thought you were away.'

'Not now old boy,' he said.

He did not offer to call my wife. The silence lengthened.

'Is Susan there?' I said eventually.

'She'd like to see you,' said Saul. He sounded like a marriage guidance counsellor.

'Well shall I come down?' I said.

'Do . . . ' said Saul.

I supposed this was the way he sold houses. Ella wasn't very keen on the idea. She kept talking about toffee-nosed children and people with plums in their mouths. I could understand her position, I said, but they were my children and if she didn't mind . . . . She said she didn't mind it was just that I was such a remote stuck-up bastard. I said I knew I was but wasn't she in her way a difficult person to . . . etc etc. Then we started to discuss our sex life. Then I got drunk and went to bed.

I looked in on Paul Tucker before I went to tell him about my encounter with Ainsworth. He wouldn't tell me what Ainsworth's indiscretion was, and at the end of the encounter I came to the conclusion that Tucker did not even know himself.

'He'll tell us soon enough,' said Paul.

'Why?'

'Because,' he said, 'soon there'll be nothing left to play for. Soon there'll be Prothero and his friends and that is all there'll be.'

'Ever heard of a company called Amtro. Property Company.'

'No. Why?'

'Harry Ainsworth mentioned it.'

'He confides in you more than in me then.'

Ella didn't want to come. She said she had had enough of 'all that'. In the evenings now we didn't talk. I sat and watched her and thought. She was drinking just over half a bottle of gin a night. There had been a time, just before

Abbott was killed, when I had suspected her, but not now. I thought she was telling the truth about Abbott. All the motives for the murders pointed away from those intimately concerned with Peace and towards someone with enough to scare the life out of both of them. Someone with powerful connections. Someone like . . . Ray Prothero. As I watched Ella not watching me, I began to wonder whether my interest in her was purely professional. The less I thought of her as guilty the less I felt I needed her. We didn't even sleep in the same room now.

It was curious though. Just occasionally, often when I had been out on my own and was on my way to the flat, I felt watched. Perhaps it was a legacy of looking out that night to see Abbott on the pavement opposite, perhaps it was just because no-one had thrown anything at me for weeks and I was beginning to wonder why.

It was a bright, clear day when I went down the A22 towards Susan's new house. I had dressed for the occasion. I was wearing my one good suit and a blue tie. I had invented a current assignment to impress them all. 'I've been offered six weeks to look after a rich American businessman. Very good money.' I even had a name for the businessman in case they asked. But, by the time I turned the Cortina into Saul's drive, I had begun to wonder whether even guarding an American businessman was enough. What would I have to do to impress those two? Look like them I supposed. Look as happy to be in this right little, tight little island as they were.

Susan was in the kitchen waving brass saucepans about the place. Saul was in something called his 'den'.

'Shall we just chuck a lump of raw meat in there and leave him to it?' I said.

Susan gave a silvery laugh.

'I didn't understand your last letter,' I said.

'Why not?'

'Oh I understand the words. I just couldn't understand why you'd bothered to use any of them.'

She turned to me, framed against the window, a chunk of the Sussex landscape around her like a halo. She looked as if she was about to endorse some domestic product.

'You were always saying I was a snob Charlie. Christ, look at you. If people don't slide around making cracks and looking as if they've just walked out of some Hollywood film of the forties you don't want to know. Everything about you is a pose. Every move you make. Yes I'm sorry. I'm not particularly clever or unstable if you want to know. I want a nice home for my children and someone who'll look after me and probably my letters strike you as stupid and naive. But not everyone can walk around looking rumpled and bruised and doing impressions of Humphrey Bogart all the time.'

I got up and tried not to look as if I was trying to look like Humphrey Bogart. This was, for me, quite difficult and I don't think I managed it. I liked her again, and that wasn't easy either. I'd been looking for ways to dislike her, of course. Looking for things that wouldn't hurt me. And now Ella and I were finished, I could see, quite clearly, all the things that had drawn me to Susan.

'I'm sorry,' I said.

She put her arms round me.

'Me too.'

At this moment Saul put his head round the door.

'Hullo you two,' he said.

'Hi!' I said.

I determined to be charming. There was, I saw, something doggily eager to please about him. He was wearing a touchingly casual pullover and a pair of cavalry twill trousers. Christ, I thought to myself, you're probably learning to ride.

As he took me up to his 'den' – a room that had the air of resolute maleness adopted by commercials for after-shave – I wondered, after all, whether Saul wasn't as scared as me or any of us. This place was probably bought on a mortgage he couldn't afford. This pathetic aping of the local gentry – who were presumably all people who were busy aping him – was just part of that defeated charade we were all playing. Communists, nouveaux riches, journalists, detectives – we were like some out-of-season carnival, the hopeless children of a banana republic.

'Dry sherry old boy?' said Saul.

'That would be very nice.'

He went past the leather chair and, from the bookcase, which, I noted, contained the complete works of Dickens, took a heavily bound copy of *The Brothers Karamazov*. He opened it to reveal a bottle of sherry and two glasses. I found I was laughing helplessly.

'Good, innit?' said Saul.

And now we were both laughing. Everything about the room had suddenly struck my as hysterically funny.

'Don't tell me,' I said, 'there's a tequila sunrise inside *Oliver Twist* . . . . '

He poured us both a drink.

'What do you *do* exactly Saul?'

'I buy and sell, old boy' he said.

'Yes.'

A thought struck me.

'Tell me – have you ever heard of a property company called Amtro?'

Saul paused and looked professional.

'I have,' he said, 'as a matter of fact I have.'

'What do they do?'

Now we were discussing business, he had relaxed. He sat at the heavy, carved desk waving his glass expansively, man to man, in the den.

'They're international. They're plugged into God knows what. Enormous resources. Their speciality is buying up companies on the slide and not wasting valuable money trying to do anything with them. Run by an Australian called Grant.'

I decided not to indulge in a discussion of the ethics of property speculation.

'You're a mine of information Saul.'

'Why do you want to know?'

I told him a heavily edited version of what Ainsworth had told me.

'Look,' he said, 'I know Grant. In the way of business. I'll give him a ring if you like and tell him you'd like to see him.'

'Thanks.'

Saul grinned.

'Do I tell him you're a private detective? He'd love that.'

'Tell him . . . .'

Saul put his feet on the desk. He was wearing an expensive-looking pair of brown shoes. I had a sudden vision of my children growing up here. Of them learning to call him 'Daddy'. Of them acquiring his vowels and values. Maybe I am a snob, I thought. I don't like cheap, nasty, empty things. I don't like you, Saul.

'I'll tell him you want a job,' he said. And laughed.

The brief moment of companionship was over. I went to the window. Down on the lawn I could see Ben and Toby. Susan was out there too, Rupert in her arms. She seemed to have changed clothes again. Clearly in this house one changed to go out into the garden. Saul probably had a jacket to go with each brand of cigarette.

'Ben!'

All I wanted was for him to look up. He ran off across the lawn.

'Ben!'

'He can't hear you old boy I'm afraid. The den is soundproofed.'

I looked down at his figure. There was probably no crying or screaming in this house. But maybe no scenes of passionate reconciliation as there had been between myself and each of my children. It was all very tidy and ordered and controlled. Perhaps that was better.

'I wasn't much of a father,' I said.

'No?'

'I was drunk a lot of the time. And I wasn't there you see. My father wasn't there.'

'Fathers,' said Saul, 'are supposed to be there.'

'Yes,' I said.

I found I was beating against the glass, my fists hammering at it as I looked down into the sunlit garden.

'BEN! BEN! BE-EN!!'

But the soundproofing, like everything else in that house, had been done thoroughly and with care. My son didn't hear me.

Mr. Grant of Amtro Property (U.K.) Ltd. lived on a yacht. This, Saul, informed me with a chuckle, was for tax purposes.

'Where is this yacht?' I said.

'All over the place, old boy,' said Saul. 'This week it's down by Tower Bridge.'

He had made me an appointment for the following Monday.

'Do you want to come?' I said to Ella.

'No,' she said, 'you're wasting your time.'

She had been to the doctor, she said, and the doctor had given her some pills. She took three a day. They made her look as if she was suffering from concussion.

I tried to tell her what I was doing. She wasn't interested. All she said was,

'You're wasting your time.'

I went anyway.

I was met at the pier by two small Filipinos in white dress uniforms. They bowed low and asked me to step into their launch. I asked them whether they made the uniforms themselves. They told me that they did not. The launch was big enough for a family of three. As we cut through the water I saw the huge white sides of a boat ahead of us.

'Does Mr. Grant ever come ashore?' I said.

'Mr. Grant', said one of them 'is on dry land very very infrequently.'

There were even more Filipinos to greet us when we got to the yacht. They were hanging over the sides of the boat grinning eagerly. I asked the smaller of my escorts what they did.

'They help Mr. Grant to do it,' he said.

I wondered whether they were a formation dance team.

'No,' said the one who was driving, 'all are fully qualified professional sailors.'

I was taken along the side of the boat and shown into a

large cabin. On a table by the door was a huge pamphlet labelled AMTRO GROUP: AN INTRODUCTION. Judging from the quality of the paper this was no ordinary pamphlet but they clearly hadn't spent a lot on the writer. 'In the last year,' he began, 'Amtro consolidated its position worldwide as . . . .' As a bunch of crooks presumably. There were then a lot of figures with a ludicrous amount of noughts in them. I looked in vain for a picture of Mr. Grant or his yacht. When he came in I was surprised. I don't know why, but I always expect very rich people to be old. This man was in his late thirties, wearing an open shirt, a blazer and a peaked hat. All he needed was a megaphone and he could have walked into a job at Butlin's. He smirked at me and offered me a drink. I tried to smirk back.

'I have a friend,' I said, 'who says you should always audition the company.'

He smirked again. Saul had provided me with an amazingly elaborate biography, taking a pleasure I found surprised me in working out the details of what he called 'our little hoax'. I was, apparently, something called a 'high-flier'.

'Your friend is right,' said Mr. Grant. 'Tell me about yourself.'

I told him about my company and what a good year we'd had. I told him of the restrictions on operations in Europe. I told him any number of lies which he seemed to regard as indistinguishable from the sort of things that happened to him every day. Somebody once said that a businessman is only a crook behind a desk. This businessman was a crook behind a desk on a *boat*, and he had the true entrepreneur's gullibility and appetite for fantasy. Eventually I got round to Newlands.

'Tell me,' I said, 'how things are going at Newlands.'

'We're bidding,' he said, 'as I suppose you heard.'

'Yes,' I said.

'And I think,' he said, 'we'll be O.K. now.'

'Yes,' I said.

'We had some opposition from inside but . . . . '

'Sure.'

Some grotty little shop steward who thought that England should be run on the lines of Bulgaria.

'You're looking for . . . . '

'For participation.'

'Yes.'

That was about as much as I got out of him. 'Just go in there and chat,' Saul had said. These people spent their time 'just chatting'. Chatting about deals, about places that might be up for sale, about whole factories, towns probably, they might want to buy. As I went back in the launch I saw a figure on the bank. He was wearing a smarter coat than I remembered but I knew the face at once. It was Ray Prothero.

Try this for size, I said to my imaginary assistant on the way back to the flat. The imaginary assistant was called Jake. He weighed four hundred pounds (or something like that) and was devoted to me. I had saved his life in Korea.

'You got a theory boss?' he said, his dumb eyes lighting up.

'A property company has heard the Newlands car firm is on the slide. They hear the government is maybe selling off bits of it. A *lot* of money to be made. Only this isn't like issuing shares for what was once a publicly owned company. This is real. There are men working there, there are huge warehouses, the lot. That's what these guys want to get their hands on.'

'Go on boss,' said Jake eagerly. I was getting bored with Jake. He would have to go.

'Well,' I said, 'they don't want opposition inside the plant. They don't want fuss. The main union up there is the D.W.U. And they want them sweet. So Mr. Grant and Mr. Prothero put their heads together. They cobble up a scheme to get rid of the left executive. Amtro puts up the money for the court case. Fine. Not only that though. The district organiser up at Newlands is a good old trades unionist. He can still just about get the men out even when they realise they're on a loser. So they put pressure on him.'

'How boss?' said Jake, his eyes shining.

I was fed up with Jake's eyes shining and lighting up. I wished his ears would make a noise like an alarm bell or his teeth explode.

'I don't know yet. But a little shop steward rumbles them. So he has to be killed. And Mr. Abbott, who's doing the leg work for them knows Too Much. So he has to be killed as well.'

'Jeez boss,' said Jake, 'dese property spekkerlaters sure is rough guys to play ball with.'

'They will stop at nothing,' I said.

I looked up. I had stopped at a red light and the woman in the next car was looking at me oddly. I realised I had been talking aloud. I screwed my index finger into the side of my head and gave her a gay, insane smile. She looked away. This, at least, was the first theory I had come up with that had anything like a credible motive for murder in it. After all, if the crime wasn't a domestic affair, there would have to be more involved than the internal politics of the D.W.U. And the selling off of a large company like Newlands was obviously big money.

I have often noticed that we view the world exclusively through the narrow lens of our current enthusiasms. Motorcyclists see nothing but motor bikes. For young mothers, the streets are full of babies, and for Charles Alexander, at the moment, every newspaper and television programme seemed to be discussing the state of play up at Newlands. On this particular evening, Paul Tucker was giving his expert views on the future of the company.

'The new leadership,' he said, 'have said that they will make compromises. That means . . . . '

What he seemed to be saying was that all the D.W.U. members were going to be fired and the D.W.U. executive weren't going to do anything about it. But he didn't say it like that. It was curious how English public life altered the language one used. I could no more connect this bland, authoritative figure on the screen with the man I knew than I could that slumped figure in the Indian resturant with someone called COMMUNIST BOSS OF NEWLANDS PLANT. I gazed at him blearily, wondering how I would begin to trace out the long line between Stan Peace and Prothero. Whether I would ever be able to make any of it stick.

Ella came in from her room.

'Turn it off,' she said.

'No,' I said.

Had she been drinking as well as taking those pills.

'Please,' she said.

'No,' I said.

'Fucking unions,' she said, 'fucking load of useless fucking men wasting their fucking time. I never 'ad no union. I never 'ad fuck all. All I ever done was sit in and listen to people like you and Stan go on and on and on about things I didn't give a fuck about.'

'I thought we weren't allowed to talk about Stan.'

'Tonight we are,' she said.

'Prothero – ' I began.

'Don't give me that, Charlie. Prothero? What are you on abaht? Prothero? Oo's Prothero? Jus' some union cunt. Oh look in front of your fucking face Charles and see what is there? Don't give me this shit about Prothero. Can't you see? Can't you see it?'

I turned the television up as loud as it would go.

'Are you saying you killed him?'

'I've got a fucking good idea who did,' she said.

On the screen Tucker was talking about lame ducks and people going to the wall. About the need for recovery, about the up-turn in the economy. Behind all these stale phrases, I thought, were lives. With each sentence I heard futures closing. Ella was crying.

'YOU DON'T KNOW!' she was saying. 'YOU DON'T KNOW!'

No I didn't know. Not about her. Not any more. Maybe she was another statistic, best described in the sort of words that a social worker would have understood. Maybe she was a disturbed one-parent family and I was somebody who tried to live his life by a code learned from books he'd read thirty years ago. She wasn't a lovely lady and I wasn't a private eye. They don't let you do things like that any more. The man interviewing Tucker was talking about compassion.

'I'm going out,' I said.

'PLEASE CHARLIE CAN'T YOU UNDERSTAND?'

'No,' I said.

I went out into the street and walked across to the White Hart. It was well lit and there were a lot of people in there. I didn't talk to anyone, although two people tried to talk to me. All the time I could hear Tucker's voice in my head: '. . . The fact of the matter is as far as the moderate element in the union is concerned . . . '. Maybe the world was like some gigantic, senseless machine that crushed, impartially and senselessly, anyone who tried to stand for long enough. The crime wasn't the murder. The crime was in being alive at all.

When I got back all the lights in the flat were on. The television was still going. They were talking about Beirut now. I couldn't see Ella anywhere. I went in to Tommy's room. The boy was asleep. There was nothing in his room either, I noticed, apart from a few books I had bought him.

I went back into the sitting room. On the screen was a picture of a shattered building with a woman crying in the foreground. I turned down the sound. Then I heard the tap.

She was lying, naked, in the bath. She had hacked at her throat with a razor blade with clumsy passion, and the water was dyed red. It wasn't that that had killed her though. She had swallowed practically the whole of her latest bottle of pills, and some of my sleeping pills as well. Unlike a lot of other things in her life, she wanted to do this properly.

I know funerals are supposed to be depressing, but they always depress you in ways you had not anticipated. All weddings seem the same. Funerals are horribly individual.

The particular stroke of genius at Ella's was the vicar. A youth of about twelve, he kept using her first name every third word, like an advertising man trying to impress a client. When the box slid off on the travelator, taking the mortal remains of Ella Peace with it, he turned and gave it a sort of wondering sigh as if he were a courier, greeting an over-familiar monument with professional amazement.

The weather did quite well too. There was a howling wind round the chapel, which almost drowned the responses of the three members of the congregation. I had chosen the hymns, which included 'Blest Are the Pure in Heart'. I wished I hadn't chosen it when it came to singing it because I was crying too much to get the words out. Really one should pay a woman to come in and tear her clothes on these occasions.

Maggie came. She seemed to think a lot more highly of Ella now she had slit her throat. She stayed close to me and put her arm on mine but I didn't feel able to look at her. She seemed to me just another fat old lonely woman. It was Tommy who got me through it. His hard white face, his lip set against tears. His look of an animal who expects life to be just like this made me swear silently that no-one would take him away from me. In case some busybody from the social services had been keeping an eye on the flat or Ella should prove to have brothers and sister in unlikely places, I had decided to pretend that Ella and I were married. Not that there seemed much danger of anything like that. Like the boy in *Bleak House*, Tommy couldn't remember no uncle nor aunt nor brother nor sister.

I put my arm round him as we came out of the chapel to the accompaniment of an organ that sounded as if it were miming to a record. They had a Garden of Rest and a Place of Remembrance and a Scattering Area and a Hall of – well I can't recall what it was a Hall of. All I remember is that I didn't want ever to go back to that place where they had burned the thin, silent woman with the blonde hair. We all went over to look at the wreaths. There were three wreaths, all from me. That was it. I held Tommy's hand very tightly. As we stood there in the bitter wind I noticed another large black limousine slide up towards the chapel as if on invisible rails. Then, over by the trees that separated the crematorium from the main road, I thought I saw a figure. I stopped. I had a feeling just like the one that had shaken me that night on the estate. Only this time I didn't wait or listen. I ran towards the trees as fast as I could.

Whoever it was saw me at once and ran back towards the road. I heard shouts behind me. You're not supposed to run in graveyards. The figure had disappeared into the trees.

They weren't more than about twenty or thirty saplings, planted on a grassy rise. They probably called it the Forest of Total Recall, but you could run through it in two minutes flat. By the time I got to the other side, though, the man had vaulted over the far wall. All I saw when I got there was a car, about twenty yards down the road. I could see a figure at the wheel but that was all. I heard a panting noise behind me, looked back and saw Tommy.

'What was it?'

'Someone who couldn't keep away,' I said.

Tommy looked down the road after the car.

'One of 'er geezers,' he said.

'Did she have a lot of them?'

He looked blankly back towards the red brick chapel and the black cars.

'It was the bastard 'oo killed my Dad,' he said.

So now I watched television with Tommy. We watched *Dr. Who* and *Spiderman* and his friends and *John Craven's Newsround* and *Saturday Superstore*. We discussed the programmes exhaustively. On Saturdays we played football on the Common. When I wasn't there Maggie looked after him. A bloke I knew in Soho asked me if I would help him evict a troublesome tenant. 'Is it a nice little old lady?' I said. 'No,' he said, 'it's three huge black geezers'. I did it, with the aid of a couple of friends and was paid five hundred pounds in cash.

What really concerned me of course was the thing I was doing for love. Or for fear of my own life. I had started to add things together and come to the conclusion that Ella had meant it when she said she was my insurance policy. A week after she died someone broke into the back of the house when I was out. They smashed everything in the kitchen, pulled out the cupboard and wrote obscene words on the wall. It could have been the local youth I suppose. But there is only one in Barnes and he works for Christian Aid.

I began to get that familiar feeling when I was out sometimes too. The feeling that someone was watching me. What kind of person? Well – the kind of person who is capable of taking a blunt instrument and hammering it at the side of someone's skull for ten or fifteen minutes. The kind of person who throws bricks through windows and leaves dead bodies against the doorbell. A crazy fucking psychopath.

And, in the best tradition of such people, he doesn't mind if you know who he is (so long as you can't prove it). He likes to know you know. And he likes to know you know he likes to know you know. Which is why, every so often, he allows himself to be seen. He hovers at the edge of your field of vision, like a fault on the lens of a camera or a face on an old film, just out of focus.

That would be the same person, of course, who was still blackmailing Ainsworth. A name and an address were bothering me. A coincidence I couldn't quite place. But I knew there was a place for them. I went up to Newlands with Tucker. Ainsworth, he had told me, was trying to get them out.

'If he doesn't,' he said, 'he'll talk to you.'

'Why?'

'Nothing else left.'

I'll always remember that day of the vote. It supplied me with a piece that had been puzzling me. I won't say it was the day when I first knew for sure who had killed Stan Peace, but it was the day I began to think I knew. And I shall remember it too for the way Ainsworth looked as he came out of the gates after they had told him he could – in the words of one of the placards – take his strike and shove it up his arse.

'What I tell you three times is true.'

What I tell you four hundred million times a day 52 weeks of the year in almost every national newspaper must be true. The members of the D.W.U. had taken all the *Sun* and *Mail* editorials to heart. Their slogans and shouts might have been written by Mr. Smith. Or perhaps he just knew what the nation wanted. It certainly didn't want tired, grey-looking old Communists like Harry Ainsworth. It didn't want to fight this one.

'They've swallowed the lot,' said Ainsworth. 'Every

bloody thing. The lot. I was wasting my time.'

'Harry,' said Tucker, with extraordinary gentleness, 'come to the car.'

He talked very easily, almost without being asked. There was a man, it appeared, called Futoyov. Something in Bulgaria. Leader of their trades unions or their security services or maybe both combined, I don't remember. Futoyov knew Ainsworth. They drank together, they went to banquets together, they talked about four years plans together. It was all very fraternal.

'That's not a crime is it?' I said.

'I don't think you understand,' he said, 'what I have to put up with every day.'

'In a way,' I said.

Comrade Futoyov, on Ainsworth's last visit to the Socialist Paradise of People's Bulgaria had taken him to the opening of some feature of Bulgarian culture – a statue to the sheet metal workers of Sofia, or a film about wheat production or a snappy musical satire on American foreign policy. There had been some kids outside with placards. He didn't remember their faces, just being irritated by them. Like kids anywhere. He thought they had been moved on by the police.

They weren't just any kids, it turned out. They were a group. All they had was a duplicating machine but they were a group. They were an ideologically unacceptable bunch of Trots, Royalists and Seventh Day Adventists. Only – here was the awkward part – one of them was a poet, and now they were all in a cellar in a government building with bullets in the back of their nineteen-year-old necks. And who put them there? Futoyov.

'What's new?' I said. 'How come it starts to bother you now? Haven't they been doing this for years?'

He asked me what I thought about the thirteen unarmed civilians shot dead by my soldiers in Derry. I said I thought it was bad. He asked me what I had done about it. I said I had done nothing.

'There must,' I said, 'be some other angle.'

'They had photographs,' said Ainsworth, 'of me looking ratty at the kids, me with Futoyov, pissed as rats, arms round each other. They had pictures of the bodies of the kids. They were no more than kids, Mr. Alexander. They had letters from Futoyov to – '

'And tell me Mr. Ainsworth,' I said, 'did this shake your faith in socialism?'

He didn't rise to that. He looked bleak and old. He looked out at the lorry park and the workers streaming out of the factory gates. They didn't even have a faith in socialism to shake, I reflected.

'Who's "they"?' I said in the end. 'And how did they get these pictures? And who took them?'

Ainsworth shook his head.

'Abbott was all I dealt with. But the demands haven't stopped.'

'Someone who still wants to put pressure on the left in the Union and someone who has access to the more finely tuned internal wranglings within the Bulgars production team.'

'Uh?'

'Those pictures must be the product of someone over there who had it in for your friend Futoyov. The English papers don't worry too much about people with bullets in their necks but a *poet*. And a fucking Bulgarian poet. And a Communist union leader.'

I could see the headlines now. I DRANK WITH TORTURERS SAYS RED CHIEF. But I was also putting together coincidences from the past. Ainsworth looked at the homegoing crowds.

'We're dead Paul,' he said, 'dead.'

I told him to stop paying the money. He said he'd decided to and that was why he had seen me. I didn't like to tell him that whoever it was had been putting the squeeze on him had already got what they wanted. He got out of the car and trudged back towards the factory.

'So,' said Tucker, 'who was it?'

'Prothero,' I said. 'He wanted to do a deal with Amtro over Newlands. Didn't want anything in his way.'

'I'm quite a good liar but Tucker wasn't impressed.

'You don't believe that,' he said. 'Too complicated. This is a chain job.'

'Yes?' I said.

We went to a pub down the road for a drink. Tucker had three large gins. It turned out Tucker believed in socialism. He thought mistakes had been made but he still believed in socialism. I said it was good that the best people still believed in socialism. Socialism was far too complicated for the workers.

'What do you believe in you great big mournful brute?' said Tucker.

'Fuck all,' I said crisply.

I still had those names Mo Allen had given me. If my theory was correct, one of them might be able to check it out. I went through all the Taylors in the listed UCATT officials. There were four. The first was twenty-five. The second was dead. The third worked, so the head office told me, on a site in Fulham.

Skip Taylor was twenty-five floors up. He came down, they told me, for tea. Would I like to go up? I looked up the sides of the building and saw my man sway high above me like an insect in silhouette. I said I would wait. When he came down he turned out to be a plump man with a strong Galway accent. He seemed unhappy to be at ground level. I caught him looking round uneasily for pot-holes as we picked our way through the mud towards a low wooden shed.

'Stanley Peace . . . ,' he said, 'I remember Mr. Peace. And if anyone did for Stanley Peace it will be one of the man's lovers I expect. He had no respect for other men's wives at all.'

'What I'm after' I said, 'is a man who wasn't on the course with you. Someone who had a row over Peace's wife. He was from the town. He – '

'Ah sure,' said Mr. Taylor, 'I knew none of them from the town at all. This is thirty years ago Mr. Alexander. You've come to the wrong man.'

'I have another name' I said, 'Gab Johns.'

'Ah now,' said the man, 'Gab knew the town crowd all right. He'd know your man all right. What did you say his name was again?'

'I didn't,' I said, 'and it doesn't matter now.'

I didn't want to say the name out loud anyway. I had no proof. It was only an idea.

I rang Saul that weekend to thank him for his help on the Amtro affair. He suggested we meet for a drink. I asked him where he drank. He mentioned the name of a restaurant in Notting Hill: 'It is', he said, 'frequented by writers and artists.' I asked him how Susan was. He said she was in the garden. 'Not where,' I said, 'how?' 'There was a pause. 'By the door,' said Saul. And we both laughed.

The restaurant was not only frequented by writers and artists, it was haunted by people like Saul trying to catch them in the act of frequenting. All round us heads craned and eyes swivelled towards the door, and each time the door opened to reveal someone just as dull as us.

'Bit dull tonight,' said Saul; 'usually a lot of writers and artists frequent this place.'

'Getting a lot of leads,' I said, 'in the chase after the bastard who murdered Peace.'

'That sounds a bit heavy,' said Saul.

'Chap called Gab Johns,' I said.

'Oh yes?' said Saul.

We talked about Grant. Saul said he was a bent bastard. I asked him how much the Newlands deal was worth. He looked suddenly serious. 'Millions,' he said reverently. We didn't get round to Susan until the end of the meal. It was strange. I had thought this encounter was about something else, but now I saw very clearly that it was about me and Susan. He told me she wanted a divorce.

'Is that why you took me out to dinner?' I said.

'Can she have one?' said Saul.

'Of course,' I said, 'has she got anyone else to go to, though?'

We both laughed. We looked, I thought, like a couple of writers and artists.

I had that jumpy feeling on the way back to Barnes. As I turned off right at the Old Rangoon, the other side of Hammersmith Bridge, I was sure I saw the lights of a car just behind me. But they didn't follow me far down Lonsdale Road. Then again, when I parked the car outside the flat, I was sure I heard a noise farther down the road. But all that, of course, was just the fear that had been with me since the beginning, had gone away for a while when I was with Ella and was now back, was now with me every moment of every day, a shadow on the landscape of my life. *There's someone out there who hates you, Charlie. Someone who wants you dead.*

Well at least I had a pretty good idea who it was.

It was foolish of me to worry about who was behind me or who was on the street. They were waiting for me in the hall when I came in. I didn't stand a chance. They jumped me from the side and hit me with something hard. My last thought, before I went out cold was, 'Will these blows stop? Or will they rain on and on and on in a limitless frenzy, like the ones that battered poor Stan Peace, and plausible, luckless, friendless Mr. Abbott?'

PART FOUR

When I woke I was strapped to a bed. I was very, very cold. There was no light in the room at all. Gradually I made out the outline of a chair and a window. That was all. Then I slept. When I woke again there was light coming from the window. The chair looked much the same as it had done in the darkness. The walls, I saw were painted rough white, and outside I could see a row of trees. There was no sound coming from anywhere. There was also a large man sitting on the bed. He carried a revolver.

'I'm supposed to top you,' he said.

'Oh,' I said as politely as I could.

'But the money's not right.'

'Oh,' I said, 'if the money's not right . . . .'

'I don't like the set up either,' said the man, 'it's amateur.'

'It's very amateur,' I said.

He got up and went to the door.

'See you,' he said.

'I wondered whether – ' I began.

But before I could think of a way of framing my request he had gone. He locked the door carefully after him.

I don't know how long I was lying on that bed. It got dark again. When I woke once more it was light. And then from outside the window I heard a scratching sound. Then a voice: 'Paddy! Paddy!' I gave a shout. It wasn't a very loud shout but the dog heard it and that brought whoever it was outside close enough to the window for me to shout again. Whoever he was he was very intrepid. He broke the glass straight away. He turned out to be a man of about sixty in a pork pie hat. He didn't try and climb in but peered down at me solicitously.

'Are you all right?' he said.

It took me quite a long time to persuade him to climb in but in the end he responded to the challenge gamely. He untied me with considerable flair, and asked me whether I had been abducted by criminals.

'No,' I said, 'it was a prank.'

'Ah,' he said wisely, 'a prank.'

I seemed to be somewhere in Essex. It didn't matter to me where. All I knew was – there was a sign on the road a few miles from the cottage where I had been kept that said LONDON 70. I knew who had taken me out there. This time I was going to keep him guessing. I liked that feeling. I thought about how he would feel when he found out I had gone. Would he be afraid? Would he look over his shoulder some nights and wonder to himself whether *I* was watching *him*? I liked to think so.

A lorry took me straight into town. From Liverpool Street I went to the flat. Maggie was there, and Tom.

'Darling,' she said, 'I rang the police. They took you away in a van.'

'They did?'

'It was awful.'

Tom came in. He appeared to have been dressed by Maggie. He was wearing white jeans and a leather jerkin. He seemed cheerful.

'She got the number,' he said.

'Yes?'

'Yes,' said Maggie.

I collected my chequebook, some cash and an overnight bag.

'Maggie,' I said, 'you haven't seen me, O.K.? I'm still missing.'

'O.K.,' she said.

The first thing I had bought at Liverpool Street was a

paper and the first thing I looked for was the story of what was happening at Newlands. It was Ted Chabot's rag. The D.W.U., I was told, was suffering a 'haemorrhage' of membership since the 'damaging no confidence vote' in district organiser Harry Ainsworth. I learned from the same paper that the D.W.U. were all at yet another conference.

It was Prothero I needed to see. So I rang Tucker. He wasn't at the office.

'He's at home,' they said. 'I think he's doing the D.W.U. special Amalgamation Conference.'

'The what?'

'Search me, mate, Ask him about it.'

I rang him at home and asked him about it. He explained it to me but I couldn't claim to have understood it. The D.W.U. were getting together, it turned out with the Z.G.L. or the A.P.T.M.O. Or rather, according to Tucker, they were being absorbed. I thought of Ainsworth as he talked and of people like him. Their touching faith that institutions are immutable. That leaders of institutions mean what they say. Then I said,

'Will Prothero be there?'

'Your murder suspect?'

'I didn't say that.'

A pause.

'If you want to know, Paul. I think he knows who it is. I think he's prepared to give me the name.'

'Look – '

Another pause.

'Come up to the dacha. Meet Mission Control.'

'Who's Mission Control?'

'My wife.'

Maggie waved me off. The first place they would try would be the flat. I hoped they wouldn't get rough with Maggie or the boy, but I didn't, for the moment, see any other way of doing it. Tucker lived about fifteen miles off the M1 towards Hemel Hempstead, and as I drove up the motorway the high winds that had been with us ever since we buried Ella bruised and pushed at the car. I checked the driving mirror every once in a while but no one was following me. I wasn't going to stop now until I finished.

Tucker's dacha turned out to be a pleasant detached house at the end of a cart track and his wife an unshockable woman of about my age. She had a slight Northern accent and the air of a woman who has been serving tea to difficult people, in a professional capacity, for some years.

'At least it's not the Scottish T.U.C.,' she said grimly as she passed me a plate of toast.

'What happens there?' I said.

'Drunkenness', said Tucker, 'beastly and foul drunkenness.'

As we ate, for almost the first time we began to share information. Not entirely. There was one conclusion I wanted to keep for myself.

'As far as I can see,' said Tucker, 'the bid for the Newlands site has been very carefully handled. It's been made by a wholly owned subsidiary of Amtro, an English operation. There'll be lots of reasons for that, mostly political. I haven't been able to find out the name of the company, because as yet no bid has been made. The rumour is that H.M.G. are smiling at the proposal, provided there aren't too many screams of protest.'

'The protest being because – '

'Because it would mean the virtual end of car production in Newlands, with the loss of thousands of jobs. No wonder they wanted to make bloody sure the D.W.U. were emasculated.'

I asked about the purpose of the conference.

'The conference is about that emasculation. The D.W.U.

membership would be absorbed into other unions with no particular history of involvement at the plant. They might have had the bollocks to fight off the Amtro bid. But it's a bit late for that now.'

The conference was indistinguishable from the last one I had been to. They could have been the same people sitting up on the platform. The interruptions and speeches could have been the same, and the faces in the hall, lifted up as at a prayer meeting, took me back to that first encounter with Abbott, and my first glimpse of the world that had meant so much to Stanley Peace.

It was held, for reasons best known to the organisers, in Hull. In a drab, cavernous place called The Royal Nettleton Halls. Nettleton, apparently, was an engineer who died of a brain tumour at the peak of his career, and the grateful townsfolk had erected this dump in loving memory of him.

'Where does one eat in Hull?' I said to Tucker as we listened to Mr. Prothero describe the need to unite and fight and struggle for the right of somebody to do something or other.

'On the train out,' said Tucker.

As far as I could tell from the conference, Prothero was going to get his deal. He had been offered, Tucker told me, as had most of his Executive, decent employment with the union into which the D.W.U. was to be absorbed.

'Unlike the vast majority of his members,' said Tucker sourly, 'Ray will be working in the New Year.'

We caught up with him in his hotel room. He looked, as he crouched over a Teasmade in the corner of the room, like some trapped animal. Seen from close quarters there was something dingy and sad about him. He seemed quite happy to talk about the Newlands deal.

'We have been assured,' he said, 'that Amtro have links with a Tokyo-based company who will ensure the continued production of cars at the Newlands plant. You have to face the fact that job losses are inevitable in this – '

I didn't want to listen to any of this. I was going to read it in five-foot letters in the newspapers anyway.

'I just want the name of the subsidiary company,' I said.

He winced.

'Am I obliged to – '

'Listen,' I said, 'someone's been getting very heavy. A lot too heavy for you and Grant. I imagine you'd be quite glad to get rid of him. You could operate through someone else. This guy happens to be a 24-carat crazy.'

'Who – '

Tucker's tongue was hanging out.

'You see,' I said to Prothero, 'I thought this case was all about politics. I thought it was men in trilbies doing deals and killing for them. But this country isn't like that. The killings were personal. And they are from my end, O.K.?'

Prothero was amused by this. He looked from Paul to me and from me to Paul. There's nothing more a good politician likes than to see his enemies disagreeing. And, whatever else he was, Prothero was a good politician.

'The name of this person being . . . ,' he said.

I wrote on a sheet of paper and gave it to him. He looked at it, gave it back to me and I put it in my pocket.

'The name of the company is Newline Properties,' he said.

I didn't stay in the room longer than I had to. Tucker followed me out into the foyer of the hotel.

'Who the hell is . . . .'

'As I said, Paul,' I shouted back at him, as I headed for the station, 'this is personal.'

'I hate to remind you of those much maligned men in blue,' said Tucker, 'but before you start getting personal – '

I stopped. He walked over to me. With a shock I realised that, in spite of his too professional manner, the odd discord between his beliefs and the way he lived his life, I liked Paul Tucker very much indeed.

'All right you stupid obstinate apolitical bastard,' he said. 'Sometime ago you mentioned some comrades who were on a course with Peace. There was an electrician. Name of Gab Johns. Do you still want him?'

'He may well', I said, 'provide corroborative evidence. You know. That stuff you don't need to print stories.'

Tucker handed me a sheet of paper.

'Let me know how you get on,' he said.

'I will,' I said.

I drove out of Hull at about midday, along the flat wastes by the estuary, the winter light lying across the water, transfiguring the huge steel bridge outside the city. I drove fast, Tucker's scrap of paper on the seat behind me. At the first telephone box I came to I rang Susan and asked if I could see her.

'Thing is,' I said, 'is Saul there?'

'Would it upset you to see him?' she said solicitously.

Susan has a touching belief that the emotional dilemmas of all her acqaintances must be related in some way to her. I tried to sound as if the sight of Saul would make me burst into tears, and she told me he was away on business. I said I would see her that afternoon or evening.

I stopped off in north London at the house of a man I used to know in the Army. As he was doing ten years for armed robbery, he wasn't in to greet me, but his wife lent me the gun. I'd like to be able to say what make it was, to make me sound more professional but I don't know much about guns. On the rare occasions when I have had to use them I just point them at whatever it is I don't like and pull the trigger. It seems to work O.K.

I got into Sussex about nine. Saul's house was equipped with a floodlight and, since the last time I'd been there, a gate that was opened from inside the house. All it needed really was a drawbridge.

'How have you been?' Susan said earnestly.

She'd heard about Ella. That didn't surprise me as much as it might have done a few months earlier. She wanted to know all the details. I didn't give her any. But later, over a drink, she got the story out of me. She put her arms round me and told me she only wanted to see me find happiness. Sometimes she had doubts about Saul. He was away so much. He could be . . . odd . . . .

'Oh?' I said.

While she was making me some supper I went upstairs to the bedroom. Ben and Toby were asleep in her bed, their arms round each other. I kissed them both.

On the mantlepiece beside them was a group of pictures. I'd remembered them from my last visit. I skipped the one of Susan aged three and the one of Susan aged twenty-five, and even the one of Susan and Saul taken a few months ago, near where he had first met her. I took the one of Saul aged about twenty, looking out at the camera with a knowing expression, looking like a not very effective version of the young Elvis Presley. It was nice the way they'd documented their lives. It was a real help.

She wanted me to stay the night but I said I couldn't. After a few glasses of wine she even put her arms round me and asked me about my 'problems'.

'Impotence?' I said. 'It doesn't worry me. I find it makes me more gentle and loving and understanding of women's sexual needs.'

'Why are you so hard on yourself, Charlie?' she said.

'It's not just me,' I said. 'I'm hard on everyone.'

I took the road that led away from the house to the east. When I got back to London I rang Maggie and asked her if anyone had been to see me. She said someone had. 'He wasn't very nice,' she said. I went to a hotel in Bayswater and registered as a Mr. Daish from Liverpool. Then, early next morning I drove out to the television company where Mr. Johns had found employment as an electrician. I was there at nine thirty. I parked the Cortina in a side street and, hands deep in my pockets, strolled up to the barred gate. There was a man in a commissionaire's uniform next to it in a kind of glass hut. I gave him a cheery wave and he waved back.

It took me longer than I had expected, to find the electrical stores, and longer still to find anyone who knew Gab Jones. Finally I was led into a back room where a fat man was soldering wire together.

'He's in the yard,' he said. 'It's funny.'

'What's funny?'

'There was two blokes just now asking after him.'

I ran out into the yard. It was crowded with vehicles most of which were being loaded with lights and equipment for the day's work. I saw Johns straight away. He was being hustled into a van up by the gates. It was being done very professionally, but he was being hustled. I ran up after the van as it pulled up to the barrier, and, as it drew away, I dashed for the Cortina. The commissionaire let the barrier go up. Maybe by now, I thought, they had him on the floor of the vehicle. Luckily, the road was blocked with traffic and I had time to turn the car round before the van pulled out and accelerated away.

Whether they had had him on the floor before, by now Mr. Johns was up and fighting. I recalled the words of that man with the gun in the empty house where I had woken strapped to the bed: 'This is a very amateur operation.'

They turned off at the first roundabout up a road that led away from the built-up area and towards the scrubby fields and small factories visible across the brow of the next hill. I was right behind them now, with both headlights blazing and the horn at full blast. If the road had been any wider I would have pulled out and forced them to the side, but, as it was, they blocked any attempt to overtake. I started to ram the back of the vehicle. Once. Twice. Three times. I realised I was screaming at them.

The road went up quite steeply after a few hundred yards, and, at the steepest part of the incline, the van turned off sharply to the left. I turned too, and found we were travelling over rough ground. I didn't leave the tail of the van. All the way across the open field I would let them get ahead and then roar into them from behind. Their driver had lost his nerve. What he should have done was brake sharply. The van was twice as heavy as the saloon and I probably would have gone through the windscreen. But he wasn't that kind of driver. I shoved at the thing in front of me like some enraged animal, harder and harder and harder, until finally, it veered off to the left, crashed through the fence bordering the far side of the field and, spinning round full circle, came to rest on a level patch of mud, opposite a stretch of muddy canal. I braked too and the two vehicles faced each other like animals at the opening stages of some ritual fight.

I drove straight at the damn thing. I was crazy with rage. I was leaning over the wheel yelling, like a Goth on the rampage, daring the bastard to stay where he was. At the very last moment, the van moved. I overshot it, braked hard and heard its engine running. Well well well, I thought, you're catching on. He was very easy to read. I let him line up on me nicely, and when I was sure he was on course I reversed back hard. As he swung round after me, I hammered the Cortina back into first and drove off at a tangent to the van. As I had hoped he jerked the wheel hard round in the middle of the first turn, and the van went into a long skid across the mud.

I did the star turn this time, getting the car up as fast as it would go and, slamming on the anchors, handbrake, the lot. I spun the Cortina through 360 degrees and found myself driving towards the open flank of the van, skidding towards me through the mud as gracefully and slowly as Torville and Dean in the middle of the slow movement. I'd forgotten about Gab Johns by now. I'd forgotten about Stan Peace and the D.W.U. and my wife and children and everything in the world apart from killing the bastards in front of me.

I hit it just dead centre and it rolled over like a shot deer. It bumped and crashed and shrieked and did all the things cars do on these occasions, and then came to rest, wrong way up at the top of a short incline that led down to the canal. I got out of the car, gun in hand and went towards the van.

I was about ten yards from it when it started to slide. It went down into the water with a kind of grunt of relief. It was only then I remembered why I was there. I could see the driver. He was still at the wheel, his head at an improbable angle to his body, but of the others there was no trace. I started down the hill but the van was already in the water. The grime of the canal closed over it like a grateful accomplice. It was only then I heard the cry. From about twenty yards behind me.

He wasn't hurt at all. He got to his feet as I walked back across the mud and I knew at once from his expression that he was the man I wanted.

'Mr. Johns,' I said, 'are you Mr. Johns?'

'What,' said the man, 'the fuck is all this about?'

'I just want to jog your memory,' I said.

Newline Properties had an office in Chelsea, which I thought was highly suspicious. They were behind Sloane Square. When I drove there later that afternoon, I reflected that, in many ways, England was becoming a more advanced country. Once upon a time a man like Gab Johns would have been aching to enter the nearest police station in order to recount his exciting experiences to them. Now he was acutely aware that such a course of action would result in the woodentops arresting him. I didn't even have to pay him to keep quiet. All he wanted was a lift back to the yard.

The Royal Court Theatre was showing a play called *Significance*. I think that was the title anyway. It may have been an extract from one of the reviews. Susan had always liked the Royal Court.

Newline were in a neat, Georgian terrace, with an entryphone. I pressed the buzzer and waited. 'Hullo?' said a voice. I was leaning towards the speaker when I felt a pressure in the small of the back.

'Stick 'em up, pardner,' said a voice.

It was Saul. I turned round and tried to smile. He was grinning.

'Fancy meeting you here,' he said.

'I've come to see someone,' I said.

'Yes,' said Saul, 'I have dealings with them. They're rather a bent bunch in fact.'

'Hullo?' said a voice.

I leaned back towards the microphone.

'They're not in,' said Saul. 'I just tried.'

'Ah.'

He made up the first fingers of his right hand into a gun and beamed like a schoolboy.

'BANG,' he said, 'BANG BANG!'

At this point a young and attractive woman put her head round the door. She seemed surprised to see Saul.

‘Oh,’ she said, ‘I thought you’d gone Mr. Newham.’

‘Still here,’ said Saul, still beaming. ‘Let me take you for a drink, Charles.’

I decided I didn’t need to go in. I was all for finishing things off neatly, but on this occasion the proper course was to go for a drink. Saul led the way through a narrow alley, chatting vociferously about Newline. They were, he said, on the way out. They were universally despised and hated in the trade.

‘Over-extended,’ he said, ‘hopelessly over-extended.’

It was curious. That prickle at the neck, that half-expressed fear I had been living with for nearly four months had gone. I felt light-headed, irresponsible and, for the first time since I could remember for ages, happy. There is a special pleasure in tracking an animal for a long way and then, at the last, watching it break and knowing that what you have to do now is almost childishly simple. There will be no more waiting, no more guessing at half-heard sounds. All you have to do is to finish it.

‘I know a nice little wine bar,’ said Saul, ‘where we can have a quiet drink.’

‘Nice,’ I said.

The wine bar was full of people who had just been to see *Significance*. Judging from the shell-shocked expressions on their faces, they had found it extremely significant. Saul led me to a table in the corner and, unbidden, bought us a bottle of Frascati.

‘Well old boy,’ he said, when we were half way down the first glass, ‘how are your enquiries going along?’

‘Fine,’ I said, ‘I think I’ve tracked down the murderous psychopathic bastard who did for Stan Peace. And Dave Abbott come to that.’

‘Who he?’ said Saul.

‘And’, I said, ‘Ella.’

Saul looked concerned.

'That was awful, old boy,' he said, 'that was an awful thing to happen to anyone. We were so sorry to hear about that one. Really.'

We drank a little more.

'What have you been up to today then?' he said.

'I was showing somebody a photograph,' I said, 'and I broke someone's neck.'

I was enjoying this conversation. So was Saul. He giggled in a vaguely camp way.

'Ooh that's a bit strong, old boy,' he said.

'Yes.'

He looked round the wine bar, packed tight with men in suits and what looked like a crack regiment of Sloane Rangers. This was Saul's country. He beamed at me delightedly.

'Well,' I said, 'the trouble is . . . I don't know what to do with this information really.'

Saul looked worried.

'I suppose,' he said, 'in these cases it is very difficult to prove anything.'

I played with the stem of my wineglass.

'I think the Anglo-Saxon system was best really,' I said. 'You know – if you murder a man's wife he can have your ear. Or vice versa.'

'Bit difficult to implement,' said Saul.

'Oh these days,' I said, 'no-one bothers about the police. Don't you agree?'

Saul agreed. The Sloane Rangers and the men in suits were headed back for a little more significance.

'I'll tell you what, old boy,' he said. 'Come down this weekend. We'd love to see you.'

'Thanks,' I said, 'I will.'

And finished my wine. I liked that 'we'. I wondered what he was going to do with Susan.

I figured it was safe to go back to the flat now. Everything was very clear and very simple.

When I got there I found Maggie and Tommy playing pontoon.

'Does he go to school or anything?' I said to her.

'School,' she said, 'is a lot of Cock.'

There were a number of messages on the answering machine including one from Tucker.

'Harry says,' he said, 'that if you can find out who killed Peace and if that information is of any use to him, by which I mean that it could be used against the people who have, I am not using the word lightly, Charlie, *destroyed* him, then it is your duty to communicate it to us.'

He read this like an American President making an announcement on television. When I read the evening paper I understood why. The Newline bid for the Newlands site had been made public. The Government also, said the story, was 'having serious talks' with a Tokyo-based company. Governments, of course, have to be seen to act decisively, like policemen. Anyone who knows anything about it knows that they take what's on offer, and if it's on offer from an international property company – fine. Did I have a duty to talk to Ainsworth? Was I being absurd in my refusal to involve anyone else?

'Do you believe in duty Maggie?' I said.

'Duty to who darling?'

'Oh just . . . duty. You know.'

'Sort of generalised obedience you mean?'

Tommy got up and switched on the television.

'I mean. Somebody thinks I should tell him something.'

'Who is this someone?'

'A journalist.'

'Journalists always think that darling. They think they've got copyright on free speech. Trouble is they have.'

I poured us both a drink and watched Tommy's thin

white face, absorbed in the glow of the screen. I thought I knew where my duty lay. Later on, in bed, alone and unable to sleep I resurrected Jake. I put him in a pair of white silk pyjamas and had him come round the door of my room to check on me. Like all good manservants he was worried if I didn't sleep.

'Jake,' I said, 'I'm not a real private eye.'

'Did dose boys say sumting nasty to yer, boss?' he said.

'I mean,' I said, 'if I was a real private eye I would just go down there and blast the bastard's head off. You know?'

'You are a real private eye, boss,' said Jake. 'It's dese good taste Limeys gettin' to yer again. You're too god for 'em. Go down there and goddam blast him, boss. If dat's what yer wants ter do.'

'I do,' I said, 'I do.'

Saul hadn't said precisely when I was to come. That was all part of the fun. I parked the car about a hundred yards down the road and by-passed the automatic gate. He had the place fairly well protected. I had to crawl under a wire fence, and wondered briefly whether he had some sophisticated alarm system that would monitor my every move. I patted the gun in my inside pocket and crawled forward across the damp ground.

It was about eleven in the morning when I got there. When I was about a hundred yards from the house I heard a radio at full volume from one of the upstairs rooms. Jimmy Young was asking someone about their career. I inched forward and looked up at the window. I saw Saul looking out from behind the glass. It was curious. It was as if I had never really seen him before. Oh I'd seen the shoes and the hair-style and the mannerisms and the expensive car and all the other things I had come to dislike so much, but now, for the first time, I actually saw his *face*. It was not the sharpness of the features that caught my attention, or the cunning little tilt to the chin, it was the way he seemed to be modelling himself to his reflection. It was that look of limitless narcissism that caught me, a look that said,

'I'm crazy, Charles. I'm the craziest thing you'll ever see. I'm as crazy as you are. Come and fucking get me.'

I was sure he wouldn't have anyone else in the house. That didn't fit. But I was also fairly certain he'd be armed. I waited in the undergrowth. After a while he moved away from the window, nice and slowly. I went on crawling forward. There were some outbuildings about thirty yards to the left, a series of gently sloping roofs that led into the side of the house. I was covered all the way there.

When I reached the outbuildings, I pulled myself up on to the roof and slithered up towards the second stretch of tiles. These, like the first, were sloping. There was then a flat stretch and a vertical wall of about nine feet. Fortunately, along the left end of this, was a solid looking drainpipe. I pulled myself up it, and hauled all shaking fifteen stone of me up on to the last ledge before the house.

I was looking at a window that seemed to have been designed to go round some internationally famous work of art. It was all thick ribbed glass and steel bands. The kind of thing that would require ten men and a diamond drill to get through it. It had, however, one great advantage to the housebreaker. It was open.

Oh, I thought, that's it is it?

Nevertheless I swung myself in onto the carpeted corridor, without a sound. I was still unable to work out quite what it was he had in mind. Was there somebody waiting for me in one of the rooms off this passage? Too simple, I decided. Not right for this stage of the proceedings. *Know your man. He's like you in many respects. He reads the same stories, goes after the same women.* In the distance I could hear the radio. It was playing a sickly sweet country song. A man loved a woman and he just couldn't tell her that the woman wasn't her no more . . . . I went down the corridor.

Saul's house, in fine mock-Tudor style, had a kind of minstrels' gallery on the first floor off which were three or four bedrooms. All of these doors, I saw when I came to the end of the corridor, were open. The music was coming from the one on the far right, and, as I reached the gallery, someone turned it louder. I started towards the room, gun in hand. At each doorway, I will confess, I was waiting to be pulled in by some hand, or to feel the shock of a blow, like the blow that had laid me out in the flat.

But it didn't happen like that. When I got to the room from where the noise was coming, I saw straight into it. Saul was standing in the centre of the wide expanse of carpet. He was wearing a blue blazer and a white polo neck sweater. He looked really pleased to see me.

'Oh my word, old boy,' he said, 'you've got a *gun* . . . .'

'Jump der guy,' said Jake. *'Don't take no shit like dat from him.'*

I didn't of course. I stood there wondering at the cool assurance on Saul's face.

'You pinched a photo of me, old boy,' he said.

'Yes,' I said, 'I had to confirm that you knew Peace and Ella at Ruskin all those years ago. He remembered you.'

'I thought he might,' said Saul, 'that's why I tried to approach him.'

'What were you doing there?'

'I sort of ran a pub,' said Saul with a grin, 'knocking shop really.'

'Yes,' I said, 'shall we go into the garden?'

Saul grinned.

'If you'd like to,' he said.

'MOVE!' I said.

He moved, but slowly, and in a way that made it quite clear that he was only going because he fancied the walk. We went round the minstrels' gallery and down past the boudoir, through the summer hall, out past the cocktail area and through a heavy door, next to which was a pile of mud-soaked boots.

'I don't think you ought to shoot me,' said Saul, 'because I've told some reliable people I'm here, and I rang them when I saw you arrive.'

I pushed him out on to the lawn. He kept on walking, towards the swings and the climbing frame that I supposed my children would be expected to use when the summer came. Well summer was never going to come. Not for Saul Newham.

'Turn round,' I said.

He turned, prettily. In some ways, I decided, he had a babyish face. The protruding ears, the air of having recently been scrubbed by a pumice stone gave it a sort of knowing innocence. I remembered that day I had driven Ella down here, and the way she had stopped as soon as she realised where we were going. She must have had the shock of her life.

'You left me alone after Ella moved in with me, didn't you?' I said.

'Well,' said Saul, 'I knew where to find you. She told me how you were doing. I made sure she did. She and I go back a long way. We're a similar class of person, you see.'

'She was terrified of you that was all.'

Saul grinned easily.

'You think so?'

I waved the gun at him. He looked down at it. It didn't seem to affect him much.

'It was Julie's place that started me off,' I said. 'You see I'm a great believer in coincidence. But I had a fairly good idea it was one of our Bulgarian friends who had had a go at me on that occasion. No particular reason. Just didn't like being followed. But *why was he there*?'

'I recommended it,' said Saul.

He was pleased about this as well.

'That's where you picked up the Futoyov photos wasn't it?' I said.

'The chaps from the socialist countries drink there,' said Saul, 'murdering bunch of bastards.'

'You gave the Futoyov photos to Abbott didn't you? You remembered him from a long way back.'

'I have a very good memory for people,' said Saul.

He shivered slightly. I didn't move. I wanted to get to him. I wanted to see that mask of self-assurance crack. Only for an instant. But I wanted to see some trace of . . . of a man, I suppose. Under the blazer and the neat shirts, inside the cars and the practised smile, there must be *something*. I wanted to see what it was. He was still smirking as I said,

'Newline is your company. You were in hock to Grant. Maybe owed him money I don't know. What you wanted to do most of all was to impress. That's what you like to do, isn't it Saul? So you told Grant you were bristling with contacts inside Newlands. You could sew the unions up for him. Maybe he believed you, I don't know.'

'We set it all up nicely,' said Saul. 'We got Ainsworth a little perturbed. We got – '

I interrupted him. He didn't like being interrupted.

'That's what I couldn't understand. None of this was strictly *necessary*. Most things would have gone the way of Amtro and its friends anyway. That's how this country runs. There was someone there with a fancy mind, giving things a crazy little shove.'

He didn't rise to this. I went on.

'Murder is a domestic crime for the most part. I was looking for someone who hated Peace, who loathed him enough to batter him again and again and again. You'd never forgiven him for that business with Ella in Oxford.'

'I loathed that little fucker,' he said, 'a narrow-minded, tight-arsed little sod. I loathed him.'

'And he loathed you,' I said, 'that night I found him at the flat. "Newham" not "Knew him". He was trying to say your name.'

As he relived the events of that night, Saul's face darkened.

'It was me on the stairs,' he said, 'I'd come back for the address book. I got the shock of my young life when I saw you.'

'That's the only thing I can't work out. I can see why you wanted the book back once you knew I'd got it. Maybe Stan had ringed your name with arrows and minus marks I don't know. What I don't see is how he got my name in the first place.'

Saul started to laugh. It began as a sort of physical fault in the lower jaw and, by degrees, spread to the cheeks and the lips. From there, quite naturally, it reached those baby blue eyes and erupted into what looked like genuine, spontaneous laughter. You had to hand it to Saul. He was crazy in the grand manner.

'Well, of course, Charles. *I* made sure Stan Peace got your name. At the beginning of the Newlands business I'd got some people round to frighten him. And I'd heard about you from Susan. What a joke. A private eye. We don't *have* those any more. We have policemen and criminals and they get on with it by themselves. They leave everybody else alone. The only way to stay alive these days is not to get involved with either of them. I gave your name to Abbott to give to Peace. They were still speaking to each other in those days, because Peace hadn't rumbled him . . . .'

'But when he did,' I said, 'you said you'd handle it. Abbott was happy to leave it to you. But he was scared when he found out what a crazy he was dealing with. Which is why he talked to me. I was his insurance policy.'

'Some insurance policy,' said Saul. 'Yes, I got you into that address book. I like the people in my life to coincide.'

I knew what I was going to do now. My manner relaxed. Not that Saul noticed that. He was in a world of his own. If I was happy, he was happy. He probably thought I was about to shake hands and apologise.

'What I don't get,' I said, 'is why you left me alone for so long?'

'Well,' he said, 'I didn't know how much you might have. I thought you might be quite good you see.'

'I've got plenty of things that confirmed it to me,' I said; 'your name on the list of directors at Newline. I've got the man Ella called He with a capital H. I've got – '

He cut at the air impatiently.

'Oh you're fine,' he said, 'you've got a few words spoken by a dying man. A photograph, years old, of someone. Your name in someone's address book. What have the police got? A few bodies, assault and battery, and after that a lot of dead history. Some people who were at . . . where is it? Ruskin College? You've got a very private solution.'

I stepped towards him. The wind stirred the expensive-looking copse of trees behind him. He didn't flinch.

'Ella was seeing you all the time wasn't she?' I said.

'All the time,' said Saul, 'she'd leave you to see me. I'd never lost touch with her even after I got lucky. You never got Ella. You got a shell, a picture, the sort of thing tarts give to soldiers. She told you absolutely fucking nothing. Because all the time she was with you, she was with me. In reality, she was with me. Because you can't satisfy a woman can you, Charles? You live on pure fantasy. On air. Ella told me. Susan told me. Not much cop between the sheets. One of those useless fucking romantics.'

He put his face close to mine.

'You haven't got anything but circumstantial fucking evidence,' he said.

I fired the gun six times. Each time I aimed it just past his left ear. To his credit he didn't move an inch. When the gun was empty I started to hit him. I hit him in the face first, then I hit him in the stomach. After that I hit him in the groin. It wasn't much fun.

I don't know what it was he had in his pocket. By this time, I was beginning to assume I would go on and on hitting him until he coughed up blood or said he was sorry. But it didn't happen quite like that. He hit me hard across the back of the neck with something metallic and, bent double, loped off across the grass. I went after him.

The two of us ran woozily across his well-manicured lawn. At the far end of it was a hedge. Someone had got to work on it and each section represented a different animal. We ended up beneath a gigantic green cockerel. I got my hands round his neck and began to squeeze as hard as I could. Saul brought his knee up into my stomach and I let go. Then he broke free and ran away through the gardens.

Here they were stone, ornamental walks. Every few yards was a crumbling, artificial pool. I was still working out the details as I stumbled after him. Of course, Saul was broke, desperate for money. Who had told Peace that it was Saul behind the pressure on Ainsworth? Abbott presumably. Or Ella. Either way it hadn't taken Saul long to trace the danger. Maybe he had been over there with Ella. Peace had walked in and . . . .

The details didn't matter. Ella. I still had this picture of her in the bath that night she killed herself. I remembered the desperation on her face . . . . ' . . . I do love you Charlie . . . .' The way she'd looked that first time I'd gone to see her on the estate and she thought I had been sent by Saul. That look of blind fear. He was good at that. At scaring people so much they couldn't even confide in big dependable Charles Alexander.

I caught him at the end of the stone gardens. I went for his legs in a great, sprawling dive and he fell heavily on to the rough grass beyond the walk. The two of us rolled together down the slope, punching kicking scratching biting, and then came to rest on a sodden clump of grass. I rolled over on top of him and started to hammer at his chest. He lay still. But there was no strength to my blows any more. I hit him again and again and again, but the blows didn't seem to connect. He was still motionless. For a brief moment I thought he was unconscious and then I saw him looking at me. One, unwinking, baby blue eye. He was crazy. Just stark, staring crazy. What can you do with people like that?

Unsteadily I got up and went back towards the house. When I was about fifteen yards away, he propped himself up on one arm and shouted,

'You've got your solution Mr. Detective. Now get out.'

I was going.

It wasn't until I was half way down the drive that I heard

the police car. That two-note wail, so familiar in the city, practically the lullaby of the sreets and houses I knew, sounded fresh and strange in the cold, bright morning. There were two cars, parked on the other side of the gate and three nice policemen in shiny black uniforms were studying the lock in a helpless sort of way. They looked cunning when they saw me. There was blood across my face and down my coat and I was wheezing like a pensioner in heavy fog.

'Mr. Newham?' one of them said.

'Who wants him?'

'It's in connection with an assault,' said his companion.

I gaped at them.

'On who?'

'On a Mr. Charles Alexander,' said the first one.

I started to laugh. The first policeman was enjoying this. He even got out a notebook. With an air of immense control, he said,

'We have reason to believe that the vehicle AJK 340 is – '

I continued to laugh. Of course! The van that had taken me away that night. Maggie had got the number. Tracing cars is one thing the police do understand. I was still laughing as the policeman adjusted his face to an 'It'll be the worse for you sonny expression.

'Come on,' I said, 'I will lead you to him.'

Perfect crimes should involve as few people as possible. Saul's taste for the bizarre and extravagant was, really, his only mistake. They had found the man who was driving that night. He was wanted on another charge. He was willing to incriminate Saul. He was willing, as far as I could see, to incriminate anybody. I considered myself very lucky not to be accused of planning my own abduction. I didn't tell the police the whole story. I didn't think it was their kind of thing, but I told them enough to suggest that Saul might have been involved in Peace's death. There were interviews and more interviews. At one point I thought they were going to hold me, but, in the end, it was Saul who stayed behind. He didn't seem worried.

I had several debts to discharge. First – early the next morning – I called Tucker. He was, his wife told me, out at Newlands. I drove straight there.

There were three pubs near the factory, and he and Smith turned out to be in the first, along with Chabot and half a dozen other tired and ill-looking men.

'What's up?'

'Don't you read the papers?' said Tucker.

He passed me three. It wasn't headline news but all three made mention of the talks between Newlands management, the Kyandisho company of Japan and Newline Limited.

'What happens,' I said, 'when they find out that the director of Newline is in stir on account he tried to have me done over?'

Tucker yawned.

'Not a lot,' he said, 'there are three other directors, and they're all clean. Anyway that story's wrong. Newline are out of the bid. Since your display to Mr. Prothero, they came out of the closet.'

'I don't understand.'

'Well it was only an attempt to look a little better. What does Newline matter to them?'

He looked weary.

'To have your gesture make any impact you should have waited. Let Mr. Newham get stuck into the talks and then give them everything you had.'

'I didn't have anything,' I said, 'it was pure luck they got him on anything.'

I felt empty and useless.

'And how did you get on to Newham?'

'I did some research on the directors of Newline. When I rang your friend at home I got your ex-wife. After that . . . . '

I didn't want to think about Saul now. I was thinking about my last conversation with Maggie. Duty. Well if my duty was to myself, I hadn't done it had I? I looked at Tucker.

'So where is the D.W.U. in all of this?' I said.

'The D.W.U.', he said, 'is gone. It's gone the way of Mr. Peace. Prothero's been absorbed.'

'While his members', said Smith, 'are to be replaced by robots. As most of them are indistinguishable from robots anyway.'

'No wonder,' said Chabot grimly, 'they fucking elected him.'

Tucker had another gin. He was in a talkative mood (it appeared the parties concerned with the Amtro deal were liable to be locked in a boardroom for the rest of the day). He told me the D.W.U. was a classic illustration of a very old rule. Without an effective trades union, workers were going to be ripped to bits by management.

'It's not that simple,' I said. 'If the section of the workforce represented by people like Ainsworth had any bargaining power, that is to say if they were still any use in the company's terms, then the strikes and the rhetoric would mean something. But in that case the company wouldn't have been planning to make them redundant would they?'

Everyone had views on this of varying degrees of complexity. Chabot, it turned out, was something called a Daleyite, which sounded to me like a rare mineral. Tucker did not join in this discussion. Instead, when it had died down, he pointed to a figure in the far corner of the pub. It was one of those huge, well appointed places, with every sort of entertainment promised, from live music to a gigantic fishtank. Over by the fishtank, in a solitary chair, sat the man with the over-bluff face and the two tufts of devil's hair behind the ears. Harry Ainsworth.

'What's he doing here?' I said.

'He's getting drunk,' said Tucker. 'Come on. You can tell him about your friend Newham.'

We went over to Ainsworth.

'Hullo Harry,' said Tucker.

'Hullo,' said Ainsworth.

He looked at me blearily.

'Oh,' he said, 'it's you.'

'Afraid so,' I said.

'When I came into the motor industry,' said Ainsworth, 'if you had a union card you didn't bloody work. Christ we only won negotiating rights at Newlands in '47. And now – you'd think we were some kind of bloody Mafia.'

'Have you had any word?' said Tucker.

'Well it's all over,' said Ainsworth, 'the deal is done. The semi-skilled workers at Newlands are now represented by unions who do not give a stuff about them. I – '

He was very drunk. Looking at him sitting there I could begin to understand how he might find himself, literally as well as figuratively, in the arms of someone like Futoyov. Tucker told him my news. He seemed pleased. Rather more impressed, in fact than I was.

'That,' he said, 'is valuable information.'

'It's – '

'It's bloody amazing,' he said.

And then, after Tucker had bought him another drink, he began to make a speech. It was more than bloody amazing. It was bloody incredible. The working class would be able to make use of this information. The working class would make capital out of the fact that someone in Newline was bent, that some bent capitalist bastard had murdered a fine man, yes, a fine man, Mr. Alexander. They would make so much class capital that Mr. Prothero would not know what had hit him.

'Well,' I said, 'you'll have made better use of the information than me then.'

'Don't put yourself down, young man,' he said, 'you – '

He stopped suddenly as if abashed by what he was about to say, but he was drunk enough to decide to continue.

'You are a private detective.'

It sounded even more ludicrous pronounced in a solemn, drunken Northern accent.

'You find out things.'

'That fits in with your theories.'

He gave me the quick, sideways glance of the disconcerted drunk. Then he was back to the speech. It was going to be fine. They would get up off the floor and struggle against whatever it was they had to struggle against. As he spoke I had a glimpse of another, younger man, the man in those old black and white films of Mo Allen's. A man who had been once able to preach and convert. When he had finished the speech he started to sing, rapping the sides of the table. I didn't know the song. It sounded like an export version of *Greensleeves*. But some of the words caught me.

'What is it?' I said to Tucker.

'It's a Chartist song,' said Tucker. 'He always sings it when he's pissed.'

The chorus was quite catchy. I forget the words now. Something about being low, being very very low and down at the landlord's feet. 'We're not too low the grain the grow, but too low the bread to eat . . . .'

The journalists at the other table enjoyed it. One by one they drifted over to us. Somebody bought another round of drinks. And, gradually, the representatives of the capitalist press, picked up the chorus . . . . 'We're not too low the grain to grow, but too low the bread to eat . . . . We're *not* . . . There was hardly anyone else in the pub.

Ainsworth didn't stop. He sang the same verse over and over again, his face crimson with the effort. He was singing away failure. He was gloriously ignoring the evidence of his own eyes. In many ways, I thought to myself, you and I, Mr. Ainsworth, have a great deal in common. As soon as I could, I slipped away from the group and went out into the late afternoon, the shapes of the lorries against the sky and the Newlands plant, a wasteland of corrugated iron shacks, huge, hangar-like buildings. Our ugly, practical, Victorian legacy, I thought.

Susan had been staying with her mother. Now is not the time or place to discuss Susan's mother, except to say that she lives in Leatherhead. I had called twice since leaving Saul's place but on each occasion had been told she was out. By her mother. It was Susan's mother, who at the wedding, leaned forward in her pew and gave a sort of incredulous bark when I promised to cherish her daughter. I phoned her from near Newlands and told her I had to speak to her daughter. I wasn't about to abuse her or steal my children. I just wanted to talk to her.

'She's gone,' said her mother triumphantly, 'to Him.'

I rang the Sussex police and told them to call her. They had charged Saul that afternoon. I drove straight down there from the factory.

The first person I saw when I came up to the drive was Ben. He was on a bicycle.

'Hullo,' he said.

I asked him what he had been doing.

'Playing,' he said.

He was looking at me thoughtfully.

'Saul's gone away,' he said.

'Yes?'

'Mum says you're horrible.'

'I don't expect she means it,' I said.

'She does,' said Ben.

The automatic gate was open, which wasn't like her. I couldn't guess how she had reacted. Or how much she had known already.

'Do you love us?' said Ben in a small, detached voice.

'Yes,' I said.

The two of us went back up the drive.

'Some dinosaurs', he said, 'were meat eaters.'

'Yes?'

'And some ate grass.'

'Is that right?'

'Are we meat eaters?'

'We have a choice.'

The front door opened. Susan was wearing an expensive black dress. The sort you would wear to a cocktail party. I couldn't think why she was wearing it at first. Then I realised. She must have dressed up for the return. Only to find her old man was inside.

'What have we got to talk about, I wonder?' she said.

'We could find something,' I said.

In a way of course, Saul was right. Ella was a shadow to me. There had been nothing between us except an unsatisfied hunger for the way things might have been. The word 'love' is used very frequently on such occasions, to provide some justification for their fragility. What I felt for Susan was the complicated ties of shared history, and my need to deny it was, I suppose, an expression of its importance. We were lost now, looking at each other.

'Let's eat,' I said, 'let's – '

She gave me a look of pure hatred.

'All right,' she said, 'take us all to Julie's place. Saul and I go there a lot.'

'Don't argue,' said Ben, 'please don't argue.'

We went in my car. The children found a lot to criticise in the way in which it had been maintained.

'This,' Toby said, 'is a pooey car. Saul's car is not a pooey car but this is a pooey car.'

'And it's a pooey man driving it,' I said.

They liked that. Well, I've always been able to rustle up a cheap joke.

Susan sat nervously on the edge of her seat, as if frightened close contact with the vehilce would contaminate her. Neat Sussex parcels of expensive land flashed by. It was late February now. Not too long to Spring.

'Perfect, wasn't it?' said Susan.

'What?'

'Almost as good as the butler doing it really. Was it revenge?'

'Everything's revenge.'

'Tying things up. Making them neat and presentable. So as you understand them.'

I looked out at the scenery.

'He killed people, Susan. He as good as killed Ella. He was – '

'Is,' said Susan, 'is is is is. I don't know what to believe anyway. I've never believed anything you said about anything. You say you're a detective. Where's your badge? Where's your detective's clothes and your detective's office? The children know about all that. You're not a detective, Charlie. You're just a man who takes jobs occasionally.'

Her existential doubt about me didn't bother me. I was good on existential doubt. I knew I didn't go to dances for private detectives. I was aware I wasn't in the Yellow Pages. What I couldn't explain to her was this feeling, perhaps as shadowy as the passion I felt for poor Ella Peace, that I was as much a private detective as anything else. Crime is an individual passion, for those who commit it and those who solve it. I realised, as we came round the bend to the familiar windowed expanse, that in some ways I was closer to Saul than to her, closer to Saul than any of them.

'Well, call this a job then,' I said.

'You're a cold bastard, Charlie.'

'Am I?'

'Listen to the way you said that. You are as cold and as curious about yourself as you are about other people. "Am I a cold bastard?" "Ohhhhh yes maybe I am . . . ".'

She was annoyed about the photographs. I could tell that. Maybe Saul had told her an edited account of his involvement with Peace and the Amtro deal. She would have believed whatever he had told her. The fact that I might have found out the truth was irrelevant. She didn't want the truth. She wanted someone to look after her and those three innocent faces in the back seat of my car. And she had the sense to see it wasn't me.

There were a lot of things I still wanted to know but I didn't bother to ask about.

'What threw me for a long time', I said as we drove into the forecourt of the place,' was something Ella had said the first time I met her. Something about some foreigners calling round. That must have been how Peace found out about Abbott. I – '

She looked at me blankly.

'I don't know what you're talking about, Charlie,' she said. 'I really haven't a clue.'

Julie's Place hadn't changed. I looked around for men in dark suits but saw none. The place was half-empty, so I got us a table by the window. The children stared at the decor. Ben opened negotiations for a Coca-Cola. I looked at him. He was the only one really. I had shared him with her, for those first few years, until our relationship got lost between her managerial skills and my slow decline as a lover. He looked up at me and gave me the sudden, bashful smile of a child who feels himself to have been watched.

'Look, Ben,' I said.

'Where?'

'Over there. By those trees. See that horsey?'

'He's over five, Charles,' said Susan.

He had grown up so fast. I ordered a meal. It arrived with almost hostile promptness. Susan busied herself with Toby and Rupert, whose chief interest seemed to be dropping spoons on the floor and trying to see where they landed. I asked Ben about his new school. It was good he said. He was only at the Junior School but soon he would go on to the High School. I had a vision of Saul writing out banker's orders from the maximum security wing of Parkhurst. Why was I here though? I didn't belong with Tucker and the rest of them. Was that why I had come? To try and make the solution mean something? As they brought the ice cream, I put my hand on Susan's arm.

'Bit late for that isn't it, Charles?' she said.

'I – '

'We're through. Don't think you'll start it up. Ever.'

She got up.

'Don't write don't phone don't call don't speak to me. Just get away from me and get on with your grubby little business.'

'I'm so glad you feel able to rise above it,' I said, 'Next time you pick a man, why don't you try one who isn't a psychopathic murderer?'

Ben, who understood these rows almost better than we did, had cut out the intermediate stages and gone straight on to a dramatic howl.

'Please don't. Please don't – '

Susan was picking up the kids.

'Come on . . . . '

'Susan – '

But she was going. She dragged my children out through the hall of the place, all of them wailing with the shock of transition. I called something after them, but she didn't hear me. She didn't even wait in the forecourt but started off down the country road in her elegant black dress, the baby on one arm, the other two scurrying awkwardly at her heels. I stood at the window and watched them until they were out of sight but I did not attempt to stop her or to call to Ben. When they were gone I went back to my seat.

'Everything all right, sir?' said a waitress.

'Fine,' I said, 'just fine.'

Back at the flat, Maggie and Tommy were playing Monopoly. I asked again whether Tommy was planning to go to school. He said he wasn't. He seemed happy. I looked at him, bowed over the board. He was like some piece of lost luggage. All the people one would expect to know about him, appeared to have forgotten he existed. It was as if Maggie and I had claimed him and, until he committed some crime, the authorities had lost interest. I thought about how easy it was to die or disappear without anyone knowing about it, even in this protected little island. I joined in the game.

Eventually Maggie said she had to get back to her place 'to change'. Would I put Tommy to bed? I said I would. After she'd gone the two of us sat in the darkened room for some time without speaking. Then Tommy said,

'My Dad could be really nice. He could be a bastard. But he could be really nice.'

I didn't attempt to answer this. Then he said,

'Did you know my Dad?'

'In a way Tommy,' I said, 'in a way.'